Pride Publishing books by Kai Wolden

Single Books
Made of Folded Paper

MADE OF FOLDED PAPER

KAI WOLDEN

Made of Folded Paper
ISBN # 978-1-83943-794-6
©Copyright Kai Wolden 2022
Cover Art by Kelly Martin ©Copyright May 2022
Interior text design by Claire Siemaszkiewicz
Pride Publishing

Published in 2022 by Pride Publishing, United Kingdom.

Pride Publishing is an imprint of Totally Entwined Group Limited.

MADE OF
FOLDED PAPER

Dedication

This book is for trans people,
all of whom deserve to be loved.

Chapter One

I'm not sure when I first started fictionalizing my life, casting everyone around me in glamorous roles, romanticizing their flaws and my own. Maybe it was in middle school, when life was hell and it made things so much easier to imagine that the mean kids had secret, tortured home lives — neglectful parents, dead siblings, empty cupboards, holes in the roof that let in the rain. Maybe it was in high school, when I skipped class and hid in the back of the library with a stack of books, listening to the other truants who slipped between the shelves for more sensational reasons, contriving storylines for their hurried love affairs, illicit exchanges and muffled heartbroken sobs. Maybe it was after high school, those nights working at the general store, where drunks shuffled in to buy cigarettes and pornography, where my boss told me not to accept checks from Black people, where one year off to save money for college turned into another and another while at home my father slowly died from lung cancer. Regardless, at some point along the way, I developed a fascination that bordered on fetishism for tragedy.

I had always planned to go to college. There was never a time in those five years that I resigned myself, even for a moment, to a lifetime of working at the general store or the mill where my father had grudgingly labored for most of his life. I made excuses for putting it off year after year—money, my father's health, my mother's well-being after he died. She didn't need me, but I pretended she did, pretended she needed someone to clean the leaves out of the gutters and fix the leaky pipes at the very least. I put into that drafty old clapboard house all the love I was never able to give to my father and all the love I wished I could give to my mother that she wouldn't accept. When she told me she was selling the house and buying a condo in Des Moines, it was like she was telling me she was giving me up for adoption. I was twenty-three, but I curled up in the corner of my closet and cried like I was six. Then I crawled out, grabbed the laptop that I'd scrimped and saved for and lay on the threadbare carpet all night, researching colleges.

I made the economical choice—I would take general classes at a community college, a respected one as far as community colleges went, that was only an hour's drive from Des Moines. I still wasn't ready to completely sever those arterial ties with my mother that she'd clipped as easily as an umbilical cord. After two years, I would transfer to a four-year university to complete my bachelor's degree, though I wasn't sure yet where I would go or what I would study. I'd only ever loved one thing—books—but there was no money in an English degree, and I needed to make money if I ever wanted to escape Iowa for good. For those two years, in which I worked odd jobs and rented an elderly couple's basement for almost nothing, provided I helped out around the house, I tried to muster an interest in something else — accounting, real estate, law, anything lucrative and sensible.

But in the end, when I confessed to my guidance counselor that I'd failed, she said impatiently, "Hey, at least you love something. You know how many people live their whole lives and never find anything they love? Do what you love." So I started applying to English programs.

I had it in mind that I wanted to go to the East Coast — Maine, Massachusetts, New Hampshire or New York. I wanted to get out of the Midwest anyway, and there was something so gloomy and romantic about the East Coast in my mind (I'd never actually been there). But when I added up tuition and living expenses, I just couldn't make it work, no matter how many financial aid packets and possible scholarships I factored in. I wasn't a particularly impressive student on paper, though I had done well on my ACTs and written a masterful personal statement on the topic of my father's agonizing demise. I ended up applying to eight universities across the United States, chosen for the prestige of their English programs, affordability and admittedly the aesthetic of their websites. I got three letters of acceptance, and when I laid them out on the flimsy card table in my rented basement room, it was the one with the thickest paper, the blackest ink and the most elegant sigil at the top — which contained an open book, a pen, a paintbrush and a violin — that drew my eye because I'd never seen anything so beautiful with my name on it. That was how I ended up in Michigan.

I was a bit embarrassed to be starting college at twenty-five—and I did think of it as starting because, compared to Weston Academy of the Arts, my quaint little community college was less than nothing. During the long drive east, then north in my beat-up Toyota with everything I owned rattling around the back seat, I did something I hadn't done in a while—made up a backstory for myself. My father's death I would keep, but it would be a boating accident rather than cancer—much more dramatic and devastating. My mother's estrangement I would also keep, but I would lose her to grief and a pill addiction instead of apathy and a condo in Des Moines. Iowa I would abandon entirely in favor of something a bit superior—Minnesota or Illinois, perhaps—nowhere that would require an accent or change to my mannerisms. I wouldn't lie about my age, but I would explain it away—a gap year that got out of hand, a spree of reckless behavior after my father's death, a soul-searching quest across South America, a whirlwind affair with a Columbian woman (I'd taken Spanish in community college). By the time I arrived, I knew my story so well it was almost as if I'd actually lived it. But I never told it to anyone.

It turned out I'd misjudged the student population of Weston. I'd thought they would be wistful romantics like me, and they were. But the people who attended Weston were people who could have gone anywhere, but chose to slum it in Michigan because they romanticized the Midwest, small-town America and working-class, salt-of-the-earth folk like me. There was no better role I could have played than William Paine from Iowa. People called me "Iowa," and soon enough, I dropped my name and embraced the character. I began to exaggerate certain parts of myself, the parts I could tell my peers most appreciated — my ignorance and inexperience (I didn't know what Uber was, I'd never tried sushi, I'd never been to Europe), my wealth of practical knowledge (how to change a tire, how to sew on a button, how to fix a wobbly table), my poverty (my old flannel shirts and scuffed work boots, my battered Toyota with its cracked windshield, my job at the campus bookstore where I hauled boxes of textbooks and mopped muddy footprints from the floor).

I played the boy next door, blond and broad-shouldered, wholesome and hard-working, bursting with Midwestern hospitality. I exuded images of green and gold cornfields, boundless blue skies, blood-red sunsets, black storm clouds and ruinous tornados. I manifested the American Gothic — William Faulkner, Flannery O'Connor, Sherwood Anderson, Stephen Crane. I became a warped and grotesque caricature of myself, composed entirely of the qualities I had been most ashamed of and most wanted to leave behind when I started my new life. But my peers reveled in it, and I enjoyed the unfamiliar novelty of being popular, even if it was for all the wrong reasons.

Chapter Two

Since I had already earned my general credits, I was free of the freshmen and sophomores, who made me feel terribly old. Most of my classes were held in Swan Hall, a glassy modern structure that housed the English, Writing and Language departments. However, one of my courses, Introduction to Shakespeare, was held across campus in the grand, ancient performing arts building. I spent so much of my time surrounded by other insecure, pedantic English majors, it was intriguing to get a glimpse into the lives of the swaggering, ostentatious performing arts students. One of them, a gregarious thespian known as "LA," took a liking to me because we had both been nicknamed after our places of origin. He always saved me a seat beside him in the front row of class, which I wouldn't have minded except that he constantly volunteered us both to read aloud. My clumsy oration compared to his energetic, flawless delivery was humiliating. I didn't have the heart to tell him this, though. LA was sunshine in human form.

It was because of LA that I started spending time in the performing arts building even when I wasn't in class. He was always inviting me to watch his rehearsals—not just me, but everyone, including the professor. I agreed out of politeness the first time, but then I kept coming back because it really was fun. He was playing Mercutio in an upcoming production of *Romeo and Juliet,* and his lengthy, melodramatic death was undoubtedly the highlight of the show. I liked melting into the plush chairs of the cavernous auditorium and giving up my role as "Iowa" for a while to become a spectator to people whose lives seemed so much larger than my own. LA had a lot of friends from different disciplines who dropped in to see his performances, and I became acquainted with them over time. Of these, there were only two constants, who I came to understand were LA's *best* friends.

Cynic, whose real name was Cedric, but who earned his appellation with his prickly demeanor and acerbic wit, was LA's opposite in every way and was, I thought, the very embodiment of everything I'd glamorized about the East Coast—money, cashmere, cigarettes, ennui, a sharp Bostonian accent. Charlie, the only one of us who didn't have a quirky nickname, but who Cynic sometimes called by his last name, "St. James," had a habit of fading into the background beside his friends' blazing personas, which made him difficult to cast in my mind. Cynic was cordial to me in his wry way, but not friendly, and Charlie never bothered to acknowledge me at all—he hid behind his curls and gold-rimmed glasses and only ever looked up from the sheaves of paper in his lap to watch LA's performance onstage.

On opening night, LA got me a free ticket and I ended up sitting in the nosebleed seats next to Cynic. He smelled strongly of cigarette smoke and some ironic cologne, and at intermission he and Charlie disappeared and came back reeking of marijuana. I was surprised to learn that Charlie indulged in such behavior... He seemed so ascetic and bookish. I exchanged only a few polite words with Cynic, but he and Charlie murmured to each other between scenes so softly I couldn't catch a word. At one point, we both tried to use the same armrest and our arms collided in the dark, and a shock went through me as though I'd bumped into Holden Caulfield on the street because, up until that point, Cynic hadn't been any more real to me. LA died beautifully and stole the show, earning much admiration from the audience, and I found myself feeling oddly proud, for I'd begun to think of him as my friend.

After *Romeo and Juliet*, LA started working on his own project, a one-man show about his grandfather's experience in a Japanese internment camp in San Francisco during World War II. He rehearsed this on a smaller stage and invited a select few people to watch — I was honored to be one of them. It wasn't completely a one-man show. During the song and dance numbers, Cynic joined him onstage and played the piano. It was a stirring performance, I had to admit, even when LA stumbled or forgot his lines, which Charlie read to him patiently from the front row. At the end of each run, Charlie clambered onstage to join the other two, and the three of them conferred around the grand piano, sometimes running through songs again, which was how I discovered that Charlie could sing even better than LA.

Once, they conversed for so long the audience emptied and I decided I wouldn't get a chance to offer LA my praise today, so I gathered up my things and made to leave. But before I could reach the door, LA called after me, "Hey, Iowa, get up here! Settle an argument, will you?"

I complied hesitantly. I'd never been on the stage, or any stage for that matter. It seemed somehow profane for me, the watcher, to invade the sacred space reserved for the performers I watched. I climbed the steps, reeling a bit as I glanced out at the empty seats and imagined them filled with faceless strangers. LA was sitting cross-legged on the piano, barefoot, in the black tank top and leggings he usually wore for rehearsals. Cynic was lounging on the piano bench, smoking — no one was supposed to smoke in the building, but Cynic didn't seem to think earthly rules applied to him, and perhaps they didn't. Charlie, leaning on the piano, was muttering to the other two, gesturing with the papers in his hand for emphasis. As I approached, I caught the distinct words, "I just don't see why we need the white guy's perspective."

"We're in Michigan, St. James," Cynic reminded him. "*Of course* we need the white guy's perspective."

"Iowa," LA interrupted them, "what do you think? Would it be problematic if I did a Japanese accent for the show? I'm really good at it. I was practically raised by my grandparents."

I stopped an arm's length from the piano, not wanting to encroach any further on their territory. I couldn't help but agree with Charlie that my small-town rural white opinion was hardly relevant on this topic. "I don't know," I said.

Charlie made an I-told-you-so gesture, but LA persisted. "But would it make you uncomfortable? As a white person?"

I shrugged. "I guess I'd have to hear it."

Charlie groaned, and Cynic let out a bark of laughter. LA beamed and hopped down from the piano. With his typical exuberance, he delivered a comical scene from Act II in which his grandfather haggled with a shop owner, this time with a strong Japanese accent. Usually the scene made me smile, but now I was careful to keep my face neutral.

"Well?" he asked at the end, tossing his fringe of black hair to the side. "Did that make you uncomfortable?"

"A little," I admitted.

"Why?"

"Because now I'm not sure if laughing at the jokes makes me look racist."

His face settled into a thoughtful frown, and he returned to his perch on the piano, legs swinging. Charlie looked vindicated, and I couldn't help but feel a bit gratified that I'd pleased him.

"Besides, LA," he said, "if you do the accent, you're going to end up with a bunch of white people quoting your show and thinking it's okay for them to do the accent because you did."

"But *I'm* Japanese-American," LA argued.

"But you don't have an accent," Charlie returned.

There was a pause, then Cynic put in, "I'm with Charlie. I hate it when white people use AAVE."

"But you don't use AAVE," LA pointed out. "You talk like a British schoolboy."

"I can code-switch," Cynic said haughtily.

After much deliberation, LA decided that he would do one show with the accent and one show without to gauge the audience's reaction. "It's a social experiment," he insisted, and Charlie couldn't argue with that. Ultimately, both shows were a huge success though the one with the accent did induce a more tense, somber atmosphere. Those who attended both were delighted by LA's artistic choice, and it was the talk of the campus for a few days. Since Cynic was in the show, I sat next to Charlie in the front row. He watched the performance with rapt attention, stage lights glinting in his glasses, and I spotted him mouthing the words to every song. At the end of the final production, while LA and Cynic were swarmed by admirers, he stood up, slung his coat over his shoulder, half-turned back to me, and said, "You coming?" I didn't know where he was going, but I went.

It turned out there was a surprise party being thrown for LA back at his dorm. Charlie and I and a handful of thespians were going ahead to set up, while Cynic kept him distracted. It was a crisp fall night, and dead leaves skittered across the sidewalk as we walked, crunching under my boots. The thespians chattered amongst themselves, rehashing the highlights of the performance, while Charlie kept quiet and smoked. At one point, one of them accosted him and exclaimed, "That last song, Charlie! I *cried*! Seriously, you made me ruin my makeup. You have to warn me next time you write something like that."

Charlie smiled and murmured some platitude. After she left him alone, I asked, "You wrote the songs?"

"It was a group effort," he replied. "I've got the words, Cynic's got the music and LA's got the showmanship."

I was startled by the envy that pierced me suddenly. I had admired them all but never particularly envied them until that moment. I hadn't had a best friend since high school, and I'd never had friends I could create things with. It dawned on me that I might have made a terrible mistake wasting two years in community college instead of committing to a four-year program from the start. Now I was a newcomer surrounded by people who had been bound together by years of shared experiences, who had settled comfortably into their friend groups and forged bonds that would last a lifetime. They might accept me, but I would never really be one of them. I had arrived too late.

LA's dorm was on the opposite side of campus from mine, a picturesque old stone building, no bigger than a large house, covered in creeping ivy. Yellow light blazed from every window, and music and laughter assaulted me in a wave as the front door swung open. The party had started prematurely, and everyone panicked for an instant when we walked in, thinking LA was with us and the surprise was ruined. Then they returned to their festivities while the thespians blithely joined in and Charlie, who seemed annoyed, began straightening up. I helped him set up the food and drinks in the kitchen and took out the recycling, which was already overflowing with bottles, while he attacked the pile of dirty dishes in the sink. Cynic texted Charlie when they were on their way, and everyone scurried about, turning off the lights and finding hiding places. Charlie and I crouched behind a couch close to the door, and for several long minutes, the only sound was his soft breathing next to my ear.

Then the door opened and LA's voice demanded, "Why's it so dark?" The lights flicked on, and we all jumped out with a mixed, unintelligible shout. LA, ever the performer, tried to theatrically faint into Cynic's arms, but Cynic was distracted by a girl handing him a drink and failed to catch him. LA recovered quickly and began making his rounds, hugging and thanking everyone, including me, though I tried to tell him I'd played no part in the arrangements. The party resumed with more gusto than ever. I'd been to parties on campus, but not with the performing arts students. They were a rowdy, show-offish crowd, talking over each other, vaunting their talents and scrambling for the spotlight. I drifted here and there, being sucked into vivacious conversations, accepting drinks when they were offered, playing the small-town boy dazzled by the virtuosity around me. And I was dazzled.

LA was so mobbed by fans it was impossible to get anywhere near him, but I could hear his animated voice across the room as he reenacted certain parts of the show by popular request. I also heard others quoting the show and saw Charlie's fear realized as white and other non-Asian people made heinous attempts at Asian-American accents. Cynic, fueled by a steady supply of drinks from various devotees, commandeered the piano in the common room and thoroughly captivated half the guests with his thunderous and haunting renditions of popular songs, which the vocalists present were eager to sing. After an evocative performance of Adele's *Set Fire to the Rain*, he paused to gulp down a scotch and soda, and said, "Don't tell my mother, but I fucking *love* white girl music."

Charlie kept to the sidelines, fielding compliments on the show while refusing to take any credit. He drew my eye occasionally, but I didn't try to join him. I had no idea what I would say. He looked young compared to his peers, with a slight frame under his oversized sweater, sleeves rolled up so they bunched around his skinny forearms, and fine features half-hidden under his overgrown tangle of chestnut curls. I watched the way he coolly downed his drinks and wondered if he was even twenty-one. I knew he was a junior, but maybe he'd skipped a couple of grades as a kid – he seemed like that sort of genius. He was average height, but his slouched posture made him look shorter, especially when Cynic, who was well over six-foot, slung an arm around him, causing him to spill his drink, and dragged him over to the piano to sing *Mad World*.

Charlie disappeared a while after that, and Cynic got too drunk to play anymore. He weaved about, drink in hand, cigarette hanging from his lip, somehow managing to appear imposing and sophisticated in spite of his condition. Our paths crossed in the hallway, and he captured me unexpectedly, throwing a languid arm around my shoulders and leaning on me. It was surprisingly easy to support his weight – he was tall but had a rangy build and most of his height was in his legs.

"Hey," he said, breathing smoke in my face. "Idaho, right?"

"Iowa," I corrected him. The whiskey on his breath was powerful enough to make me feel drunk.

"Iowa," he repeated, drawing out the word. I couldn't tell if he was mocking my pronunciation or just slurring his words. "You're not a freshman, are you? How come I've never seen you until this semester?"

"I'm a transfer student," I told him.

"Yeah? Where'd you transfer from?"

"Community college," I said with my usual candor, but I felt a prickle of self-consciousness. Somehow I suspected Cynic wouldn't be nearly as enchanted by my humble background as the rest of the Weston student body.

"Community college," he said slowly, again leaving me unsure if he was mocking me. "And what did you learn in community college?"

"Not much," I admitted. "A bit of Spanish."

"Yeah?" He crooked a smile. "*Tus labios se ven solitos. ¿Querrían conocerse con los míos?*"

I stared at him blankly. "Okay, I guess I didn't learn anything."

He laughed. "Don't worry, I'm full of shit. I only know pick-up lines."

I laughed too, disarmed. His face, coldly handsome from a distance, was more human up close where I could see the slight dimples in his cheeks and the crinkles at the corners of his eyes when he smiled. He released me with some difficulty, patted me on the shoulder and said, "Welcome to Weston. You should come by the Blackbird sometime—that's where we hang out, Charlie, LA and me. Now, if you'll excuse me, I think I'm going to be sick. See you around, Indiana."

The party started winding down after that, and I decided it was time for me to make my exit. I stopped to say goodbye to LA, whose audience had dwindled, and he hugged me again—his head barely came up to my chin—and introduced me to the group as his friend, which warmed my heart. As I left, I spotted Cynic, apparently quite recovered, making out with a woman on the staircase.

Chapter Three

I didn't take Cynic up on his invitation for a while because he'd been so drunk, I doubted he'd meant it or even remembered it. The Blackbird Café was the more upscale alternative to the cafeteria, and I had always avoided it due to the price. But one rainy afternoon as I was passing by, I glanced through the expansive front window and saw the three of them camped out in a booth, laptops, books and mugs scattered across the tabletop. The image was so picturesque and comforting, I couldn't help but stop and stare for a minute. Then LA caught sight of me and waved, and I had no choice but to go inside. The atmosphere was vastly different from the hectic cafeteria, cozy and tranquil with the hum of murmured conversation, the tapping of fingers on keyboards, and the gentle clink of dishware.

LA looked up as I approached and exclaimed, too loudly for the hushed environment, "Iowa, thank God you're here. I have an audition tomorrow morning, and these two think they're too cool to run lines with me."

He scooted over to make room for me, almost knocking over his mug in the process, and I slid into the booth beside him.

Cynic, who was wearing sunglasses even though the day was gloomy and slumped in his seat, head resting on the back of the bench, said lazily, "Charlie thinks he's too cool to run lines with you. I'm just too fucking hungover."

Charlie, who sat across from me, nose buried in a book I'd never heard of, responded, "I just don't see why you need us to do it when you have *dozens* of overeager theater friends."

"Come on, you know how theater kids are," LA complained. "They always try to make everything about themselves!"

Cynic winced at his volume and brought a hand to his forehead. Charlie lowered his book to give LA a deadpan look. "I can't imagine what that's like."

"You'll read with me, won't you, Iowa?" LA coaxed, sliding a script in front of me. "It'll be just like Shakespeare class."

"LA, I'm really not good at this," I sighed. Somehow the prospect of reading in front of Cynic and Charlie seemed ten times more daunting than doing it in front of the entire Shakespeare class.

"You don't have to be good," LA reassured me. "I'm the one who has to be good."

"At least let him get a drink first," Cynic chimed in, coming to my rescue. "Put it on my tab. Last name's Devereux. And while you're at it, I could go for a Bloody Mary."

"Cyn, you know they don't have spirits here," Charlie reminded him. "Just wine and beer."

"I know. I came prepared this time." He patted his breast pocket and I heard a faint slosh. "Just get me a Clamato, will you?"

I complied, grateful for the distraction. It was too early for alcohol by my standards, so I ordered a coffee on Cynic's tab. By the time I returned to the table with the burning mug in one hand and ice-cold glass of Clamato in the other, Cynic had sucked LA into a rousing debate about the racial dynamics in *Hamilton*, causing him to forget about running lines with me. That was the moment I made up my mind that I liked Cynic very much.

"I'm just saying, it's ridiculous to have a white man onstage yelling at a Black man for owning slaves."

"But Lin-Manuel Miranda isn't white—he's Puerto Rican."

"Whatever, he's white-passing—like Charlie. It's an important distinction. For example, Charlie can't say the N-word, but I can."

"You've never said the N-word in your life."

"But I could if I wanted to."

"I don't think you could pull it off."

"That's racist, LA."

I sat back and enjoyed their antics while Charlie stuck earbuds in his ears in an attempt to drown them out. Outside, rain pattered on the window and students hurried past, unrecognizable under their umbrellas and hoods. I tried to imagine what we looked like to them, recalling the idyllic image I'd seen through the glass and inserting myself the way one might picture themself in a scene from their favorite movie. Eventually, the debate died out and LA remembered his upcoming audition. Cynic, having polished off his Bloody Mary, announced that he was going for a smoke and clambered across Charlie's lap instead of asking him to move, which Charlie tolerated without comment.

With Cynic gone and Charlie listening to music, I was much more comfortable running lines with LA. The play was a tempestuous romance written by one of the drama professors and was, I thought, rather terrible, but LA was determined to land the lead male role, Sam, which left me to play the part of Jessica. He read with such fervor that I was sure the people nearby thought we were having a real conversation and that we were involved in the most toxic relationship in campus history. Charlie had the grace to pretend he couldn't hear us, but at one point when Sam accused Jessica of cheating and she threw a drink in his face — which I mimed with my empty mug — I caught him smiling.

LA got the part, of course — he was unquestionably the best actor at Weston — and within the first couple weeks of rehearsal, he started dating the short, freckled redhead who played his love interest. At first I wondered how healthy this could be after watching the two of them scream at each other onstage for hours on end, but I found they were refreshingly affectionate offstage without being gratuitous.

The Blackbird became my regular haunt, thanks to Cynic's apparently limitless tab which kept me fueled with overpriced coffee, baked goods, sandwiches and, in the evenings, wine. I'd never had a rich friend before, and half the time I didn't know whether I should believe the things that came out of his mouth. He was aware of this and used it to mess with me sometimes. Once, when I reproached him for smoking in the theater, he replied, "My father paid for this building. I can do whatever I like in it." When I gaped at him in amazement, he cracked a grin and said, "I'm kidding, Iowa. Jesus."

Cynic, I learned, was an only child, like me, but his parents were divorced and his father had remarried, giving him two "God-awful white step-siblings." He was a dreadful student, was only passing his classes because of Charlie, had dropped or flunked out of three other schools previously and was actually my age. Evidently, he'd only ended up at Weston because his father had refused to keep funneling endless money into a hopeless cause. But now he was dead-set on graduating, to spite his father if nothing else. He and Charlie had been roommates their first year, while LA had lived down the hall, and the three of them had been inseparable ever since. Cynic and Charlie, I thought, had the dynamic of an old married couple, while LA was perhaps their energetic son. I might even have thought the two of them were in a relationship if I hadn't seen Cynic slipping away with women at parties so frequently.

Cynic was entirely unashamed if not proud of his utter dependence on Charlie. He was fond of announcing, "I'd be dead if it wasn't for Charlie. I owe this guy my life," while ruffling Charlie's unkempt curls. He meant it literally, I found out later, when I got the story out of LA. At a holiday party their freshman year, Cynic had given himself alcohol poisoning, passed out in a snowbank and most certainly would have died had his roommate not gone out searching for him. I must have looked concerned because LA assured me, "He was a lightweight back then."

I asked, "Have you ever tried to talk to him about it? The drinking?"

He shrugged theatrically, turning his palms to the sky. "Have you ever tried to have a serious discussion with Cynic? It's impossible. Besides, we all drink."

While this was true, I thought it was obvious that Cynic's drinking was on another level. In fact, now that I thought about it, I wasn't sure I'd ever seen him completely sober. He held it well so he got away with it. I only saw him truly wasted at parties, and even then he managed to appear unfailingly cool and collected.

LA, in contrast to Cynic and me, came from a large, close-knit family with five siblings, three older and two younger, all of whom were pursuing much more practical career choices than him. He'd ended up at Weston because his parents were convinced he only wanted to be an actor because he'd grown up in Los Angeles and were unwilling to spend any real money on his education until he deigned to study something serious. He, like Cynic, was committed to proving his parents wrong. "I'd rather die than work a single day at a desk job," he told me more than once. In the grand tradition of theater students, he planned to move to New York after college and try to make it on Broadway.

As LA and Cynic took shape as vibrant, full-fledged characters in my mind, Charlie remained muddled and obscure. He almost never talked about himself and was difficult to start a conversation with at all. Though he bantered freely with the other two, he was guarded when it came to me. I could almost see him withdrawing into his impenetrable shell when I approached. Occasionally, though, he offered up tidbits of information, seemingly by accident as if he'd forgotten my presence. Once, when I'd offered to take a look at Cynic's car, a gorgeous BMW convertible that he'd neglected to change the oil on for over a year, Charlie remarked, "My dad taught my brothers everything there is to know about cars but didn't teach me a damned thing."

"Why?" I asked him, and he glanced at me sidelong, exhaled a stream of smoke and said nothing.

Another time, when I was saying something quaint about my small-town roots, he interrupted, "So what? I'm from a small town too and you don't hear me blabbing about it all the time." I clamped my mouth shut and felt myself blush.

The one safe topic I could find common ground with him on was books. Cynic and LA didn't read much, but Charlie consumed novels at an almost alarming rate and seemed to have a new one in his possession every time I saw him. Every now and then, I got lucky and had actually read or at least heard of the book he was reading. A few times, I was even able to draw him into real conversations about them. This was somewhat nerve-racking because he lost interest so easily if I said the wrong thing, but it was also delightful because once in a while, if I said just the right thing, I was able to earn a smile.

As winter set in, LA and I started going to the campus gym for exercise. His girlfriend, Lindsay, tagged along sometimes—it was important for stage actors to keep in shape, she told me. They usually stuck to the weight room, but I'd been a swimmer in high school so I was drawn to the lap pool, which was far superior to the one in my hometown. Cynic avoided exercise at all costs, but Charlie made sporadic appearances at the gym. He once disclosed that he had run track in high school, but he was nowhere near as fast now, thanks to smoking. One day, LA and I were getting dressed in the locker room when Charlie joined us, wet from the shower, a towel draped around his slim shoulders. He faced away from me as he shimmied into his jeans, and I focused on tying my shoes. LA left abruptly to meet Lindsay, but I lingered, packing my bag.

At some point, the idea had taken root in my mind that Charlie was gay. I wasn't exactly sure what made me think this. I had never seen him with anyone or heard him mention a romantic partner. I couldn't justify it, but something about his appearance and mannerisms had me absolutely convinced. And it made me nervous, not because I was uncomfortable with it, but because I was afraid that I would inadvertently do or say something to make him think that I was uncomfortable with it. I suspected this might be the reason he was so reserved around me. My "Iowa" persona was largely constructed on my sheltered naïvety, and perhaps this had led him to believe that I might be homophobic. So I lingered even though I was ready to leave because I didn't want to give him the impression that I was uneasy being alone in the locker room with him.

I didn't look at him directly as he dried his hair with his towel, put on deodorant and pulled his T-shirt over his head. But I didn't look away either. And it caught my eye as he half-turned in my direction, a ropey pink scar that stretched from under his arm all the way across the left side of his chest. I reacted before I could stop myself, drawing in a sharp breath and exclaiming, "Charlie!"

He looked at me, pulled down his T-shirt, then muttered, "Don't treat me any differently."

I could only stare at him. With a cloudy expression, he gathered up the rest of his things and left.

Over the next few days, my imagination ran wild. My first thoughts were of some sort of horrific accident—I had visions of Charlie, bloody and unconscious, slumped in the wreckage of a mangled car. After I calmed down a bit, I realized that was unlikely. The scar was far too neat for that—it was a surgical scar, which struck me as even more ominous. A heart surgery? A transplant, even? After some gruesome research, I found that these types of scars were typically vertical, not horizontal. But still, whatever it was, surely it was dire. What had he meant by *"Don't treat me any differently"*? I racked my brains at night, unable to stop picturing the dark look on his face. Wouldn't someone have told me by now if Charlie was unwell, if his life was in danger?

I tried not to treat him any differently, but every time I saw him, I had flashbacks to hospital rooms, gurney beds, IVs and beeping monitors. My father's wheezing cough. The smell of disinfectant and death. If Charlie had been standoffish toward me before, now he was downright cold. He hid behind a book whenever I sat down in our booth at the Blackbird and came up with a reason to leave shortly after I arrived. I couldn't tell if Cynic or LA had noticed his behavior. They were his best friends so they undoubtedly knew his secret, but I could glean nothing of it from them. They didn't act like there was anything wrong with him—in fact, the way Cynic rough-housed with him sometimes made me clench my teeth with anxiety. Charlie had become a fragile thing in my mind, a delicate thing made of folded paper that might crumple at any moment or blow away in the wind.

My fears culminated one afternoon when I went to the Blackbird after class and found only Cynic, LA and Lindsay awaiting me. LA and Lindsay were running lines for their next play—since her arrival, I didn't have to do it anymore—and Cynic was drinking coffee, probably spiked with something from his trusty flask, and staring out the window. I sat next to him in Charlie's usual spot, which felt strange.

"Where's Charlie?" I asked him, attempting to keep my tone light, though a feeling of foreboding had settled over me.

"Sick," he replied. "I think he'll be out for a few days."

I had to bite my tongue to stop myself from interrogating him.

Charlie was out for more than a few days. The week that dragged by was the longest week of my life since my father's death. I confined myself to asking about him once a day, receiving only short, uninformative replies from Cynic. He didn't seem worried, but he did appear somewhat listless. He and Charlie did everything together and he was lost on his own. He asked me for help on his assignments a couple of times, but I didn't know anything about musical theory. He smoked even more than usual and got kicked out of the Blackbird twice for lighting up inside.

I couldn't focus on anything. Dread gnawed at my insides, and I was stricken by a terrible pang of loss every time I saw his empty spot at the table. It was inexplicable. I hardly knew Charlie, and we definitely weren't friends — in fact, I was fairly certain he despised me now. But when I envisioned him lying sick in bed, impossibly small under the blankets, perhaps too weak to even get a glass of water, it made my heart feel like it was riddled with shards of shrapnel. I suspect that I never fully recovered from that week of thinking Charlie was dying. It defined our relationship from then on in subtle, fundamental ways. My perspective on him shifted so profoundly, I was never able to view him the same way again. He became something more than human for me, an icon, an ideology.

When I showed up at the Blackbird to find him reading at our table as though nothing had happened, I froze in my tracks for an instant, unable to believe my eyes for I'd thoroughly convinced myself by then that I would never see him again. No one noticed my momentary loss of composure. LA and Cynic were arguing cheerfully about something, and Charlie didn't look up from his book. I slid into my seat, eyes fixed on his face. He looked a bit thinner, I thought, and maybe a few shades paler, but otherwise he was unchanged. I was the one who had changed.

"Are you feeling better?" I asked him, and his eyes flicked up from the page. They were hazel, flecked with mossy green.

"I'm fine," he said stiffly, almost suspiciously. It was the first time he'd spoken to me since that day in the locker room. I kept gazing at him, at a loss for words, until he frowned and hid his face behind his book.

His ambivalence toward me did nothing to lessen my newfound feelings of protectiveness. Although we barely interacted, I kept an eye on him, making sure that he looked all right, that he was dressed warmly enough and his color was returning. His skin, though light, had a warm, tawny undertone that was more noticeable to me in the winter when mine turned stark pale. I did my best to keep my sentiments to myself, but they burst out of me unexpectedly at times. One night when Charlie, Cynic and I were walking to the theater to see LA's latest play, Cynic stopped to flirt with a group of women, and Charlie, while waiting, lit a cigarette.

"You shouldn't smoke," I said without thinking, startled at the boldness of my words. He looked at me like I'd grown a second head, cigarette hanging forgotten from his lip. "You've been sick," I added as a justification.

He kept staring wordlessly until Cynic wrapped up his exchange and led us onward, throwing an affectionate arm around Charlie's neck as he often did. The cigarette fell from Charlie's lips to land forlornly in the wet slush, and I stepped on it as I passed.

Chapter Four

As finals week approached, the mood at the Blackbird grew more serious. Charlie and Cynic labored ceaselessly on Cynic's term papers, which Charlie refused to write for him but was clearly doing most of the heavy lifting on. He was also helping LA with his final projects, and I wondered when he had time to do his own work. Charlie's major was a self-designed mash-up of writing and music that kept him hiking back and forth across campus all day. I made the same lengthy journey, and if we were friends we could have walked together. But we weren't friends. I spotted him around Swan Hall fairly often, darting up and down the stairs, chatting with professors and pausing to examine the fluttering flyers on bulletin boards. If he saw me, he didn't acknowledge me, so I never tried to greet him.

I churned out my final papers one by one—five of them in total, which was grueling. At least LA and I were able to split the work on our Shakespeare final. We were doing a scene from *A Midsummer Night's*

Dream, which LA was bound to earn us an 'A' on, followed by a presentation of our literary analysis (my area of expertise). By the time finals week rolled around, most of my work was done, and I wandered around campus, feeling strangely bereft with no assignments to occupy my time. My job at the bookstore wouldn't resume until the spring semester, and winter break stretched ahead of me, long and aimless. I supposed I would go to Des Moines to spend Christmas with my mother and her live-in boyfriend, but I hadn't actually talked to her about it. We'd hardly exchanged more than a few texts since I'd left Iowa. Returning to my home state – which was now my namesake – didn't appeal to me in the slightest. In fact, I'd developed a crippling fear that the minute I crossed the Michigan state border, everything I'd experienced here would evaporate – LA would turn into sunlight, Cynic into smoke and Charlie into glimmering raindrops.

Our booth at the Blackbird sat empty for a few days, as my friends attended to their various responsibilities. I couldn't bring myself to sit in it alone. But on the last day before winter break, I was pleased to find the three of them gathered there, engaged in what appeared to be an intense conversation. As I drew near, LA's expressive voice once again shattered the peaceful ambiance of the café, causing other patrons to glance over in annoyance. "You lucky bastards!"

I sat down, gazing at them curiously. "What's going on?"

LA was glaring across the table at Cynic, who looked smug, and Charlie, who looked mildly embarrassed. "Cynic and Charlie are going to South America for break, and they didn't bother to tell me until now."

"It's a spur-of-the-moment trip," Cynic explained. "We were going to my mother's in New York, but she got called away to London on business, and my father's playing Stepford with his God-awful family in suburbia, so I figured why not fly south for the winter and put some of my pick-up lines to use?" He winked at me.

It didn't surprise me that Cynic and Charlie spent their breaks together as well, but I desperately wanted to ask why they couldn't go to Charlie's family. I knew almost nothing about Charlie's origins, other than the sparing hints he'd dropped here and there. I assumed based on his speech patterns that he was from the Midwest like me. He claimed to be from a small town, but I couldn't believe it was anywhere near as small as mine. He was far too academic and worldly for that. I had learned either from Cynic or LA that he had taken a year off after high school, making him twenty-two. Being the romantic I was, I had to ponder whether there was some tragic reason for his reticence about his past. Again I envisioned a car accident, or perhaps a house fire, and Charlie in a slim black suit standing before his parents' graves like Bruce Wayne.

"Anyway, LA," Cynic continued, "you're more than welcome to join us."

LA heaved a dramatic sigh. "I wish, but my mom would kill me. The whole family's coming to town for the holidays and she needs all hands on deck."

Cynic gave him a sympathetic smirk and turned his dark gaze on me. "What about you, Iowa?"

I was so stunned at the novelty of being invited on a last-minute romp to South America, I couldn't answer for a minute. It was impossible, of course — after paying next semester's tuition, I had barely a cent to my name, and while accepting Cynic's charity at the café was one thing, expecting him to fund an intercontinental trip was quite another. Not to mention Charlie's discomfort at the suggestion was palpable. He shot Cynic a sidelong look laden with such incredulity and dismay, I almost winced.

"I don't have a passport," I said. It wasn't true—I had an aunt and uncle in Ontario who I visited on occasion. But it was the simplest and least arguable excuse I could think of.

Cynic shook his head at me. "You'd better do something about that. You can't spend your entire life in this stolen, slave-built atrocity of a country."

"I've got news for you about South America," Charlie remarked. He was visibly relieved at my response.

"What are you doing for the holidays?" LA asked me with a note of something that might have been pity. They knew my background, a simplified version of it anyway—that my father had died of cancer, though not specifically lung cancer, and my mother had more or less abandoned me to start a new life with her much younger boyfriend.

I shrugged. My half-baked plans of going to Des Moines seemed at that moment too depressing to voice aloud. "Maybe I'll just hang around here," I said with an attempt at nonchalance that ended up sounding even more depressing.

LA and Cynic gaped at me with disbelief that bordered on alarm, and even Charlie glanced up at me from under his lashes for the barest instant. Once he'd recovered from his bout of shock, LA exclaimed, "No way! You should come home with me, Iowa."

Caught off guard, I protested half-heartedly that I didn't want to intrude, but he waved this aside. "Don't worry about it. My family is so big, they might not even notice you. Well, except for the fact that you're not Asian." He grew more excited as he went on, "It'll be great! We can go to parties. I'll show you around town. You can meet all my high school friends. But..." He hesitated, and I thought perhaps he'd thought of a reason I couldn't come after all. "You can't call me LA," he said finally. "You know, being called 'LA' is cool when you're the only one from LA, but when you're *in* LA, it's really, really lame. You have to call me by my real name, Elijah."

"Elijah?" I repeated in amazement. It had never occurred to me that I didn't actually know his real name. Even in the programs at his plays, he was fondly listed as 'LA.' "Jesus, I'll try but that's going to be really hard."

"I know," he sighed. "You'd better start now, to get in the habit. I'll call you by your real name to help you remember. William, right?"

"Will," I said with a smile. Warmth was growing in my chest, spreading through my veins like a shot of whiskey. But then I remembered something that made me turn cold again. "I don't have any money for a plane ticket."

Before I even finished my sentence, Cynic flourished his wallet and began shelling out cash. "How much do you need?"

Things moved quickly after that. We all bought our plane tickets and packed our bags. Cynic and Charlie left two days later for Buenos Aires, where they would start their grand tour. They didn't yet know where else they would end up. I watched them drive off in Cynic's flashy BMW with a faint pang of worry. Cynic, with his cavalier attitude and excessive substance abuse, was no doubt capable of getting himself into all sorts of trouble in a foreign country — though I was sure he was also fully capable of getting himself out of it. It was Charlie I was more concerned about, which was irrational because he was, as far as I could tell, a completely functional and self-sufficient adult. Ever since his illness, I hadn't been able to stop thinking of him as frail and somehow transient, like one of those iridescent insects that only lived for a day. I had horrible fantasies of him contracting some rare disease and languishing in an overcrowded hospital where no one spoke a word of English, or perhaps in a less tolerant country becoming the victim of a hate crime. I mentioned none of this to LA, knowing how insane it would sound.

We left for California the following day. I had only been on an airplane once before, when I was a kid and my parents splurged on a trip to Disney World. I confessed this to LA and he walked me through the security protocols without teasing me like Cynic would have. We had cocktails on the flight, and LA got a bit drunk. He was clearly anxious about going home and kept giving me instructions, which I tried my best to memorize, buzzed and giddy as I was.

"Don't mention my one-man show. My dad will think it's tasteless. And don't tell them I'm dating an actress. Actually, don't tell them I have a girlfriend at all — it'll lead to too many questions."

We made a point of calling each other by our real names as often as possible, and it felt performative, like we were reading a script. By the end of the flight, we were laughing hysterically at the silliness of the situation, irritating the other passengers to no end.

The Inoue family lived in a sprawling modern house in the suburbs of Los Angeles with massive arched windows, a meticulously kept lawn and a pool out back that was closed for the winter, though by my standards it was warm enough to swim. It was the sort of house I'd only seen on television, and I had to make a conscious effort not to appear too overawed by it. LA's parents were unperturbed by my presence. I gathered that LA had always had a lot of friends and was always bringing people home unexpectedly. They asked about Cynic (whom they called by his given name, Cedric) and seemed to idolize him as much I had when I'd first met him, which made me feel slightly inferior. They were only mildly curious about me and seemed to lose interest once they found out I came from nothing.

I had a pleasant, if slightly strained, conversation with Mrs. Inoue in the kitchen while we helped her prep food for dinner. There was one awkward moment when she joked that I ought to help her convince her son that he wasn't going to become an actor and I replied curtly, "Your son is the best actor I've ever seen." LA was facing away from me, chopping leeks, but I saw the back of his neck turn red.

The house was already full of visiting family members when we arrived, and more trickled in each day. I had been slightly nervous about being the only non-Asian, but it turned out LA's siblings had a variety of racially diverse partners, so I didn't stand out too much. LA's bedroom had been given to an aging aunt who needed to be close to the bathroom, so he and I were exiled to the pool house, which suited us just fine. It had a fully stocked bar that we helped ourselves to in the evenings, accompanied by some of the other young people who slipped out of the house after hours. We slept on a fold-out couch and woke late in the mornings to bright yellow sunlight streaming through the patio doors. LA hogged the blankets and kicked me in his sleep, and I wondered if this was what it might be like to have a brother.

LA's older brother, Jacob, who was a lawyer, loaned us his Corvette, and LA drove us all over the city, showing me everything from Hollywood Boulevard to the empty lot behind his high school where he used to skip class and smoke weed. I had to admit I felt a bit like a movie star riding around in that car, wearing a pair of aviators I'd found under the seat that had probably belonged to some wealthy, high-profile client. We went to the beach on my request — I hadn't seen the ocean since my childhood trip to Florida — and I stood knee-deep in the cold water, gazing out at the shimmering, infinite horizon. I thought of Charlie and Cynic gazing out on a different ocean in a different hemisphere, so unfathomably far away, and hoped they were having as good a time as I was. I brought back a whole beach's worth of sand in my clothing and shoes, and it rasped underfoot on the floor of the pool house and made the bed sheets scratchy.

We went to parties, as LA had promised, in houses even more awe-inspiring than his, and I met some of his high school friends who seemed more like characters from some glamorous teen drama series than real people. I swam in a marvelous, crystalline indoor pool, did kamikaze shots on a balcony overlooking the sea and drunkenly hooked up with a Valley girl, which I later regretted. On Christmas Day, I called my mother and told her where I was and that I missed her even though I wasn't sure it was true. I got a text from Cynic in Spanish that I had to use Google

Translate to decipher — it was a particularly lewd pick-up line.

After a New Year's Eve party so extravagant and hedonistic it left me exhausted for days, I started to wind down. I hung around the house and lounged on the pool deck, often accompanied by LA's younger sister, Stephanie, who was going to school for architecture but confided to me that she actually wanted to be an artist. She drew in her sketch pad while I read through the stack of books I'd brought with me, which I'd compiled from a list I'd been secretly keeping of books I'd seen Charlie reading.

The relatives cleared out gradually, LA was allowed to reclaim his room, and I was given Jacob's room after he left. It was chock-full of awards and plaques that made me feel grossly inadequate. LA fought with his parents a few times, while I kept my distance and pretended not to notice. His father mowed their lawn every other day at the crack of dawn.

We had never agreed that I would stay for the entirety of winter break, but I did and no one seemed to mind. In the final week, I was surprised and delighted when Cynic swept through the front door, looking like he was fresh off a movie set, in sunglasses and a white button-down shirt, his close-cropped curls oiled to perfection. Charlie followed, tanned a hazelnut brown, which intensified the green flecks in his eyes. When I saw him, I felt a knot in my chest loosen that I hadn't realized was there until now. His gaze passed over me, settling briefly on the cover of the book I was reading, which he had read only a month ago, and I caught a glimpse of the same bafflement on his face that I'd seen the time I'd told him not to smoke.

I expected the party-going to resume now that Cynic was here, but to my relief he and Charlie seemed as worn out by their adventure as I was by mine, and we spent a lazy, companionable week together in the suburbs. Cynic regaled us all with exotic tales of their quest, which may or may not have been true, while Mr. and Mrs. Inoue fawned over him and hung on his every word. Charlie was somewhat less hostile toward me. He seemed to recognize that the books I'd acquired were some sort of gesture, though I'm not sure either of us knew exactly what that gesture was. We still didn't talk much, but he no longer went to such great pains to avoid being alone with me, and there were a couple of nights when we sat up later than everyone else, reading in the living room in silence.

The four of us flew back to Michigan together and drove back to Weston in Cynic's car. LA had to remind me that I was now free to call him 'LA' again. I switched back easily, but from then on when we were alone together, he sometimes called me 'Will' and I sometimes called him 'Elijah' like they were private, affectionate nicknames we'd made up for one another.

.

Chapter Five

This semester I didn't have any classes in the performing arts building, but I still spent a great deal of time there. LA had been cast in another lead role, playing Jack Kelly in *Newsies*. This involved a lot of singing, which he practiced with Charlie, and dancing, which he practiced with Lindsay. These rehearsals were particularly fun to watch, thanks to the sensational dance numbers and outrageous New York accents. Cynic also had an upcoming performance to prepare for. The musicians put on a yearly concert in March that was rumored to be attended by some of the most influential individuals in the music world. Both of his parents were coming, and he bemoaned this endlessly though I suspected he was secretly looking forward to it. He shut himself up in one of the soundproof practice rooms and bowed over the piano all day, appearing every inch the musical genius, and allowing intrusions only from Charlie, LA and me.

I enjoyed seeing a side of Cynic that actually cared about something. Those prolonged practice sessions were the longest I'd ever seen him go without a drink or a cigarette. He even forgot to eat, sometimes for an entire day, so I started dropping by between classes to bring him sandwiches from the café. Food wasn't allowed in the practice rooms so he had to scarf it down while I shielded him from view lest a professor walk by. Charlie often sat in on his practice sessions for hours at a time, listening and giving him notes until each piece was perfect. When I wandered in to find the two of them sitting on the piano bench, heads close together, speaking fervidly in low tones, I found myself feeling oddly embarrassed, as if I'd walked in on a far more intimate scene.

My early speculations that there was a romantic element to Charlie and Cynic's relationship returned every now and then. For a while I had assumed Cynic to be flamboyant but straight, like LA. However, he abruptly disabused me of this notion one day with the lofty statement, "I'm a study in the dichotomy of man — biracial, bisexual and bilingual."

It was "bisexual" that grabbed my attention, but he caught me staring and I had to pretend it was something else. "You're bilingual?" I asked, hoping he didn't think his pick-up lines counted as a language.

He replied, "*Mais oui. Tout le monde devrait apprendre à parler deux langues. Le système éducatif américain est une parodie.*"

I was duly impressed. "Where did you learn French?"

"Well, my father is French," he said offhandedly. "Not that I ever learned a thing from him. I learned most of it from my au pair when I was little and a bit when I was at boarding school in England."

I didn't know what to say to that. Sometimes when I talked to Cynic, there was so little I could relate to, the conversation ground to a jarring halt.

I wasn't clear on the details, but for whatever reason, neither of his parents made it to the concert after all. He acted relieved, and maybe he was, but I was disappointed on his behalf. I sat in the audience with LA and Charlie and fantasized that we were Cynic's peculiar little family. His performance was more bewitching than I could have imagined. What I'd heard in the practice room was only a pale prelude to this dark, thunderous, enthralling exhibition. A strange paralysis settled over me while he played, cementing my feet to the floor and my arms to the armrests, and it took an exorbitant amount of effort to turn my head ever so slightly to get a glimpse of Charlie's face. He leaned forward in his seat, shoulders hunched, hands clasped between his knees, and stared up at the stage with an intensity that almost looked pained. At that moment, I had to wonder whether Charlie was in love with Cynic. If he was, I certainly would have understood it.

While I felt deliriously lucky to be accepted into their little group, I still envied my friends at times. More than anything, I envied their ability to create and collaborate with one another on their creative projects. My discipline revolved around the consumption and analysis of other people's creativity, and while I didn't regret my choice of study — it was perfect for me — I couldn't help but wish that I too was a creator. I'd always thought of myself as a spectator in other people's lives, with no more influence over the events that happened around me than I had over the plot points in the books I read. I felt like that more than ever now, and I thought wistfully that if I were an actor, a musician, a writer, a doer, then I could earn myself a central role in the group instead of watching from the sidelines. How sweet it would be to have Charlie lean over my shoulder to cast his judicious eye over my work, or to squint past blinding stage lights and see him gazing up at me with that rapt expression he reserved for Cynic and LA.

The more deeply embedded in the group I became, the more my distance from Charlie bothered me. Cynic and LA talked of us all going somewhere for spring break together, but I couldn't share their enthusiasm because I saw the uncertainty on Charlie's face. He didn't snub me outright anymore, but he was still wary and withdrawn, as if I might somehow harm him if he let me get too close. I had the vague notion that there had been some kind of misunderstanding between us, that I had missed something important, but I couldn't fathom what it might be. Something unspoken hung between us like a veil, and try as I might to grasp it, it slipped through my fingers again and again.

I honestly believe that Charlie and I would never have overcome this barrier if I hadn't started spending time with Mara, a fine arts student who lurked around the performing arts building like me because her girlfriend, Valerie, was a cellist. Mara and I bonded because we were both so obviously out of our element in those grand, soaring halls that echoed with a cacophony of voices and instruments, yet we both kept returning for the people we loved. I hadn't gotten to know very many fine arts students at Weston — they were a reclusive crowd — and I had never even been in the fine arts building. She gave me a tour of it one day and showed me her studio space, which was full of lovely half-formed sculptures of human bodies — hands, torsos, limbs and faces, none of them connected to one another. Shortly after that, she invited me over for a dinner party at her and Valerie's apartment.

The dinner was a laidback potluck affair, and the guests were mostly artists, which made for a very different atmosphere than the parties I'd become so accustomed to. We drank wine and passed around a bong, listened to soft melancholy music and talked about our favorite animated movies and our worst childhood memories. I became aware that most of the people there were gay, or queer in some way undefinable to me. They talked about it openly, using some terminology that was familiar to me and some that wasn't. The walls of the apartment were cluttered not only with art but also with various pride flags, most of which I couldn't identify. I tried not to advertise my ignorance, but it must have leaked out of me somehow because Valerie ended up walking me around the apartment, explaining the meanings of the flags. She was very tall, taller than me, which put her over six foot.

"What's this one?" I asked, indicating a pink, orange and white-striped flag that reminded me of some kind of dessert.

"The lesbian flag," she told me, blowing a kiss at Mara across the room.

"And this one?" I continued, enjoying myself. She was very kind not to make fun of me.

But at this flag, which was striped pink, blue and white, she paused and smiled bemusedly. "You really don't know this one? Aren't you friends with Charlie St. James? I always see you two together." I stared at her blankly, and her expression turned serious. "Oh, I guess I shouldn't have said that. I thought he was out."

My bewilderment only grew. We had already passed the rainbow flag, which I'd assumed would most pertain to Charlie. "It's okay. You don't have to tell me," I said, trying to memorize the pattern so I could look it up online later.

She chewed her lip for a second, then appeared to make a decision. "No. You need to know this flag if you and I are going to be friends." Then she told me what it meant.

I have to admit, even after having it explained to me by a transgender woman, I still didn't fully catch on right away. I had met trans women before and was familiar with the concept, if not the flag. But somehow I had never considered the fact that trans men also existed, or that they might not be immediately identifiable. I had simply never had a reason to think about it. Valerie must have been able to tell I was overwhelmed because she sent me some links to informative websites. It took a few hours of research for me to wrap my head around everything. Then the mortification set in.

Looking back on my interactions with Charlie in the context of my newfound knowledge, my behavior was inexcusable. I replayed the scene in the locker room again and again with increasing horror. The look on my face when I'd seen his scar must have been positively aghast. *"Don't treat me any differently,"* he'd said, and I had simply gaped at him. Then I'd proceeded to tiptoe around him like I would at the bedside of a cancer patient, shooting him endless furtive looks as I tried to deduce what exactly was wrong with him, when really nothing was wrong with him at all. My next emotion was relief so powerful it almost made me giddy. Nothing was wrong with Charlie. There was no terrible secret, no ticking clock, no malignancy in his body waiting to slowly kill him. His mysterious illness that winter had probably been the stomach bug that was going around at the time. Charlie was perfectly fine. I was just an idiot.

I knew I needed to do something to fix it, but I didn't know what. I daydreamed that some slobbering bigot would invade the Blackbird, spewing hatred, and I would heroically stand up to them in front of everyone, proving myself to Charlie as his ally. But of course, that would never happen at Weston Academy of the Arts, where half the student body was queer. Charlie wasn't on social media, so I couldn't get away with some lazy, performative online statement. Actually talking to him about it was out of the question. I couldn't even begin to visualize that conversation without breaking out in a sweat. A solution didn't present itself until the next time I ran into Mara and noticed among the many political adornments on her vest a tiny pin of the flag Valerie had introduced me to.

"Where can I get one of those?" I asked her, and she immediately took it off and dropped it into my hand.

"Keep it. I have a ton of them."

I pinned it to the front of my messenger bag, but it was very small, and Charlie made a point of not looking at me most of the time, so I had no idea when or if he would ever see it. I did get compliments on it from a few people in my classes though. Over a week had passed and I was starting to get discouraged when one day I arrived at the Blackbird before Charlie and, in a burst of boldness, set my bag down in his spot. He arrived shortly afterward, glanced down at my bag in annoyance, then picked it up and thrust it at me. And as he did so, he finally caught sight of the pin. I took my bag back, and he sat down, saying nothing. But I noticed him studying me with that perplexed expression he got whenever I made some miniscule gesture of affection toward him.

The shift in our dynamic wasn't too obvious at first. An outside observer might not have noticed anything was different. But I could sense that a door had opened, as if I'd been freezing on someone's porch for hours in midwinter and they'd finally elected to invite me inside. I started by talking to him about all the books I'd read over winter break. I'd been dying to do so. In fact, I'd taken an abundance of notes on each of them just in case I ever got the chance. He remained somewhat cautious at first, but after a while I began to see his ironclad defenses slipping. Once, as we crossed campus in a group with Cynic, LA and Lindsay, we became so absorbed in a discussion about Julie Shigekuni's *A Bridge Between Us* that we didn't notice that the other three had branched off and we'd been walking alone for the past ten minutes. At some point after that, we started making the long daily trek between Swan Hall and the performing arts building together.

Books were always our go-to conversation topic, but gradually other topics became safe for us as well — Cynic and LA's artistic pursuits, for example. Charlie loved talking about his friends' work, and so did I, even though I still felt the occasional twinge of envy. Cynic's concert had earned him mixed reviews — some felt that his performance was too edgy and unsettling, while most agreed with Charlie and me that it was brilliant. He was now working on recording some of his compositions and putting together an album for a class. "If they would quit making him write papers and just let him do what he's good at, he'd be the best student out of all of us," Charlie told me matter-of-factly. I agreed, awash with the usual sense of awe and inferiority I felt when it came to Cynic.

LA's production of *Newsies* had been such a rousing success that the video recording had actually gone viral on YouTube, earning him a flood of social media attention. He had started filming himself at rehearsals or even just eating lunch at the café to give his followers updates on his daily life. Occasionally he turned the camera on Lindsay, who enjoyed it, Cynic, who tolerated it, and Charlie and me, who hated it. Though the show was over, he still frequently adopted his roguishly charming Jack Kelly accent, which irritated Lindsay but drove his fans wild. LA and Cynic had stopped talking about our spring break plans, and I'd begun to think we weren't going anywhere after all, until one day Cynic announced that we were going to New York City and he'd already bought the plane tickets. LA screamed something unintelligible about Broadway, then launched into the chorus of *King of New York*.

We would be staying at Cynic's mother's apartment in Manhattan where she lived when she was working in the city (usually she lived in a house upstate). I didn't expect to meet her—truthfully, I'd begun to think of both Cynic's parents as transcendental beings who only existed in some bourgeois alternate dimension—but she was there when we arrived, waiting to give Cynic the keys and a brisk lecture. She was a tall, dignified woman with a well-tailored pantsuit, severe high-heeled shoes, and unapologetic dreadlocks. She had a crisp, professional manner even when talking to her son, though she did embrace him before she left and gave him a businesslike kiss on the forehead.

If LA's house had impressed me, it was nothing compared to the enormous glass-walled apartment with its lofty ceilings, gleaming hardwood floors and pristine white furniture, perched precariously on the seventieth floor of a skyscraper. The view of the city was astounding of course, but I couldn't get too close to the windows without getting vertigo. We each had our own bedroom, and though mine was the smallest, it had the plushest, most luxurious bed I'd ever slept in. There was a full bar, a grand piano in the living room and an expansive library I could have spent all day in, but we ended up spending very little time in the apartment.

We sped all over the city in yellow taxis as Cynic dragged us to all his favorite restaurants, drinking establishments and concert venues. At LA's insistence, we saw *Hamilton* on Broadway, which was magnificent, although I saw Cynic's point about the racial issues, and he and LA argued about it the whole way home. At Charlie's behest, we went to museums and the New York Public Library, which was my favorite part of the trip. When the others asked me what I wanted to do, I admitted I knew it was corny but I'd always wanted to visit the Statue of Liberty. Cynic said he wouldn't be caught dead at the Statue of Liberty, but Charlie and LA went with me while he sulked alone at a bar.

It troubled me a little, the sheer amount of money Cynic lavished on me that week. True, I'd been dining on his dime all year, and he'd paid for my flight to California, but this was an entirely different league. Between the meals, the drinks, the shows, the concerts, the museums and the plane tickets, he had no doubt spent thousands of dollars on me. I'd never had more than a couple thousand dollars to my name so I was scarcely able to comprehend this generosity. When I mentioned it to Charlie, he said, "Don't worry about it. Money is his love language. His parents showed him they loved him by shipping him off to ritzy boarding schools, so he'll show you he loves you by taking you all over the world and trying to give you everything you never had. Get a passport and get used to it."

On our last night in New York, we retired to the apartment early, where Cynic made us appallingly strong cocktails. Charlie and I perused the library and each selected the most beautiful book we could find to leaf through. Cynic plinked away on the piano in the living room, notes growing more erratic and stirring as he got drunker. LA meandered from room to sumptuous room, making videos to show off to his followers. My focus wandered from the pages of the book I'd chosen, a gorgeous first edition of *Great Expectations,* the value of which I couldn't guess at, and I found myself gazing at the dark window, which danced with mesmerizing city lights and reflected my own image and Charlie's, curled up at the other end of the couch. It all seemed illusory for an instant, a glorious fiction I'd concocted to escape the drudgery of daily life like Don Quixote. I feared that if I even blinked, it would collapse around me like a stage set, and I would find that I'd never left Iowa in the first place. So I kept my eyes open until they smarted with tears and the city lights blurred into fractals.

Chapter Six

As the weather turned warm, an air of general laziness settled over the campus. It was nothing like the end of the fall semester, when everyone had labored so diligently. Now the lawn was always dotted with splayed bodies as people neglected their responsibilities to while away the hours in the sun. Cynic stopped going to class altogether. He assured me that he'd already secured a passing grade in the only class that mattered. I worried about this until Charlie confirmed that he really was still on track to graduate next year. Even I ended up skipping class a few times, which I hadn't done since high school. I was paying so much for these courses it seemed an unforgivable crime, but there were some days when it was just so beautiful outside I couldn't make myself go, so I wound up lounging in the grass with Cynic instead, passing a joint back and forth.

We talked casually about our plans for the summer. Cynic had a new idea each day, all of which required me to get a passport, and he hassled me about it until I confessed that I already had one. Eventually, I had to tell him that I couldn't venture abroad for the summer. If I wanted to continue my studies next year, I had to work and save money for tuition. I'd already secured a job at the local middle school, tutoring summer school students in reading. Cynic struggled to grasp this and tried to talk me out of it, but I told him I was looking forward to it, which was true. I thought he would keep planning extravagant trips with Charlie and LA, but he didn't, at least not in front of me.

Mara and Valerie had put me in contact with one of their friends who had a spare room to rent for cheap, so I was planning on living there for the summer although I hadn't seen the place yet. The friend, Riley, was non-binary and used 'they/them' pronouns, which I practiced with Mara and Valerie because I wasn't used to it. Although I was confident in my summer plans, the idea of my friends leaving me behind did make my heart ache. They had become so integral in my life, the idea of going even a day without seeing them was unfathomable to me, let alone three whole months.

LA was the next one to bail on Cynic. He decided he was going to Oregon to spend the summer with Lindsay and her family. Cynic castigated him for this, saying, "What on earth are you going to do in Oregon? Drink craft beer? Go camping? Grow a beard?" LA admitted that he couldn't grow a beard and hated craft beer, but he and Lindsay had been having problems lately and he was hoping that spending the summer together would give them the chance to work through them. After this, Cynic pointedly shunned Lindsay for the rest of the week.

LA and Lindsay ended up breaking up shortly before the end of term. He didn't want to talk about it, but I could tell he was hurt. Seeing our happy-go-lucky LA dejected and quiet was heartbreaking for all of us. So Cynic decided to try to fix it the only way he knew how — with money. One day, he swept into the café and told me, "You'd better call Riley and tell them you're not renting their room."

"Why?" I asked.

"Because I got us a cabin on Lake Michigan for the summer. It's only twenty minutes out of town. I think even your shitty Toyota can handle that."

It turned out 'cabin' was an understatement. The house was designed to look like an antiquated log cabin, but it was massive, with three floors, two wraparound balconies, a hot tub and a swanky lounge in the basement with a bar, a pool table and the biggest TV I'd ever seen outside a movie theater. It was clearly meant to be rented by large groups of people, and the four of us were going to rattle around in it like coins in a dryer. Cynic suggested we resolve this problem by throwing plenty of parties. I picked a bedroom on the third floor with floor-to-ceiling windows that looked out over the lake and sat on the bed watching the sunset turn Lake Michigan into a pool of liquid fire. The trees on the property were so thick and abundant, we couldn't see our neighbors except when their boats drifted past our dock and they waved. It was pitch dark at night, beyond the wavering circle of light from our fire pit, and the stars were staggeringly bright.

We settled into a routine of domesticity that was to me both hilarious and wonderful. Charlie and Cynic played the married couple more than ever, bustling around each other in the kitchen as they prepared meals, squabbling over who had left the milk out all night and leaving each other passive aggressive sticky-notes on the refrigerator (BUY MILK—NOT CHOCOLATE from Charlie and SUCK MY DICK from Cynic). I got up for work early in the mornings before anyone else was up except Charlie, and we had coffee in the sunlit kitchen while he clacked away on his laptop. "Have a good day," he told me absently every day before I left, giving me the faint, fleeting fancy that he and I were married instead. I enjoyed my job at the school even more than I'd thought I would. The kids weren't nearly as troublesome as I remembered middle school students being when I was one of them. For the most part, they were sweet-tempered and their struggles with reading were the result of learning disabilities rather than disciplinary problems.

I was usually back by two in the afternoon, which was around the time Cynic stumbled out of bed and started roaming the house in an open robe and sunglasses to shield his hangover, cigarette in hand. "Honey, I'm home," I would call to him, and he would reply, "Hey, sweetie, I missed you."

Cynic had determined that the best way to mend LA's broken heart was by taking him to the country club down the road in the afternoons to try to pick up women. They never seemed to have much success in this endeavor and usually ended up getting horrendously drunk and needing me to come pick them up. My work schedule limited us to throwing parties on the weekends, and they were excellent parties, attended by various other Weston students who were staying in town for the summer and random people Cynic and LA met at the country club.

I knew that both Cynic and LA had one-night stands, but I didn't, even though I certainly could have. I hadn't slept with anyone since the girl in Los Angeles, and that experience had been so hollow and vacuous, I was resolved not to repeat it. While I wasn't above flirting with the women at our parties, at the end of the night I always returned to my room alone. Sometimes in the mornings, I encountered strangers tiptoeing about, using our bathrooms before they left. Once, I saw two women emerge from Cynic's room together, which turned my head, and once I saw a man, which also turned my head. But no one ever crept out of Charlie's room in the early hours of the morning, and some small part of me was glad.

While I relished almost every part of that summer, my favorite parts were the sleepy, sun-soaked afternoons when Cynic and LA had gone off to the country club and everything was blissfully still. I would swim as far out in the lake as I dared and float on my back like a dead man, letting the cold water flood my ears and swallow all sound. Then I would swim back and haul myself onto the sunbaked dock where Charlie lay with his nose in a book. Without mentioning it aloud, we had started trading off — when he finished a book, he would hand it to me, and when I finished one, I would hand it to him. Then we would wait until the other was done to talk about it. We lounged on the dock for hours each day, reading in companionable silence, or talking in sporadic bursts. And slowly our conversations began to stray from the safe boundaries we'd defined.

Little by little, Charlie pieced himself together in my mind. He was from Nebraska, a small town, but nowhere near as small as mine. His father ran a construction business, which his two older brothers worked for. His mother, a Brazilian immigrant, was a high school music teacher. He was still in communication with her but didn't speak to the rest of his family. They were staunchly Catholic. Unlike Cynic and LA, Charlie wasn't remotely rich. He'd ended up at Weston for the same reason I had—because it was affordable while still prestigious. Like me, he'd taken time off after high school to work at a local store and save money. Our lives were more similar than I could've imagined. I had far more in common with Charlie than anyone else I'd met at Weston.

There was one topic we continued to avoid—our miscommunication earlier that year. I still wasn't sure exactly what he thought had happened, and it ate away at me. At night I lay awake and planned out a million ways to broach the subject with him, but in the end I lost my courage every time. Until one particularly scorching day when I pulled myself out of the water, droplets streaking down my skin, and rummaged in the cooler we'd brought with us for a hard lemonade. It was my third one so I was perhaps feeling a bit braver than usual when I looked over at Charlie in his light blue button-down shirt, the back of which was damp with sweat.

"You know," I said, "you can take your shirt off. It's hot. You don't have to be self-conscious."

He lifted his head and regarded me from behind his sunglasses. A cigarette burned between his fingers. He only smoked occasionally, but it still bothered me a thousand times more than Cynic's ceaseless smoking. "I'm not self-conscious," he said mildly. "I just don't like people staring at me."

"But I'm the only one here," I pointed out, gesturing around us. Not a single boat was in sight. "I won't stare at you."

He let out a tiny scoff at this. "Iowa, you *always* stare at me."

I felt my cheeks grow warm and looked away quickly. I hadn't realized my attentiveness to him was that obvious. "Sorry," I mumbled after a minute.

"It's fine," he replied with a hint of amusement. "At least you stopped looking at me like I'm a circus freak."

My eyes snapped back to his face, and I opened my mouth to protest before I even knew what I was going to say. "Charlie...that day in the locker room..."

"We don't have to talk about it," he cut me off.

"We *do*," I insisted. "I need you to know... That day, I had no idea what I was looking at. I swear, I didn't even know that type of surgery was possible. I thought you'd had heart surgery or something."

He gave me a long, unreadable stare. "Seriously?"

"Yes," I answered, too relieved that I was finally saying it out loud to be embarrassed about my stupidity. "And the way you looked at me, the way you told me not to treat you any differently... Charlie, I thought it was really serious."

He kept staring for another minute, cigarette burning itself to a stub in his hand. "Jesus," he said finally. "You were acting like you'd found out I had a third arm."

"I know," I groaned. "You must've thought I was a huge bigot."

The corner of his mouth twitched. "I thought you were ignorant. Scared, maybe. I was surprised when you kept showing up at the Blackbird. I thought you'd run for the hills."

"I was so worried about you, Charlie." The words lifted such an immense weight off my chest, I was breathless for an instant.

The baffled expression I'd come to know well returned to his face. "Iowa, you hardly knew me."

"I was so worried," I repeated. "And then, when you got sick…"

He thought for a second. "Before winter break? I had the flu."

"I thought you were *dying*," I exclaimed.

He gaped at me in amazement, then, to my utter shock, Charlie burst out laughing. I'd never heard him laugh like that before. He usually laughed in soft, self-restrained huffs. It was such a wild, free, infectious laugh, I couldn't help but laugh too. Our laughter rang across the still water, and our distant neighbors must have thought we were drunk.

When he finally got a hold of himself, still gasping for breath, he said, "You told me to stop smoking. And I actually cut back."

Dizzy with elation, I suddenly confided, "My dad died from lung cancer."

His mouth fell open. "Shit, Iowa. Why didn't you tell us?"

I shrugged helplessly, and he flicked the stubby remainder of his cigarette into the water. We said nothing for a time. My insides were buzzing, the colors around me surreally bright.

At length, a smile crept across his face again. "And then you showed up with that fucking pin."

I chuckled. "You must've thought I was trying too hard."

"I did," he agreed. "But I appreciated it."

The next time I jumped into the water and swam out a few strokes, he stood up, shed his shirt and jumped in after me. I bobbed in place waiting for him to catch up, and when he reached me, he grabbed me by the shoulders and dunked me underwater. That was the first time Charlie ever touched me.

It thrilled me how comfortable he became with me after that. He would even fall asleep on the dock, head cushioned by one arm, cheek resting on the open pages of his book. Water droplets from our latest swim glistened on his bare back. He was so slight, I could've jumped from vertebrae to vertebrae or skied down the slopes of his shoulder blades if I were the size of an ant. Over time, his skin darkened to match the chestnut of his curls, and golden strands appeared in his hair. His mother was a *mestiza*, giving him a mix of South American bloodlines, while his father was white. His eyes brightened against the darkness of his skin, and when the sun caught them, the green flecks were like jewels scattered in pools of honey.

I made a conscious effort not to stare at him most of the time, but when he fell asleep I was free to admire the tiny details of his appearance—the dark fringe of his eyelashes, the careless cascade of overgrown curls, the slight outbreak of freckles on his delicate nose and the fine golden hairs on his lithe limbs. His scars were not nearly as noticeable as I'd thought. At first, I had to try not to focus on them, for fear that he would catch me looking, but soon I no longer had to try because I'd more or less forgotten about them. Truthfully, that entire summer, I scarcely gave a thought to the ways Charlie's body was different from mine. But I did think about his body a great deal.

As the summer dwindled, a hazy sense of melancholy overtook me. The days slipped by so quickly like water through my hands. Though I knew we would all return to school together, I couldn't shake the feeling that I was losing something. The Charlie I knew there was so different from the Charlie I'd come to know here. This feeling was particularly strong one drowsy afternoon when we sprawled on the dock, languid from all the hard lemonades we'd drunk. He lay on his back, eyes closed, face relaxed, but I knew he wasn't sleeping. His lips were slightly parted, and the lower one had a tiny bit of moisture on it from his last sip of lemonade. I propped myself up on one arm, gazing at him, and after a minute he opened his verdant eyes.

"What?" he asked sleepily. "Is there a bug on me?"

"No," I replied.

Then I leaned over, slowly enough that he would have time to pull away if he wanted to — but he didn't — and kissed him. To my stunned delight, he kissed me back, opening his mouth to accept my tongue. His lips were warm, and I tasted the sour-sweetness of lemonade, the saltiness of sweat and the faint bitter tang of sunscreen. Something strange happened in my chest, some sort of convulsion I'd never felt before, and a wild crescendo of heartbeats thundered in my ears. Tingles spread throughout my limbs, every hair on my body standing on end. I felt as though I'd jammed a fork into an electrical socket. My hand reached out of its own accord to grasp the back of his neck, pulling him deeper into the kiss and twisting his curls between my fingers. He made a suggestive little noise in his throat that practically drove me out of my mind. But then he put a light hand on my chest and pushed me gently but firmly away.

"What are you doing?" he asked with a trace of his old suspicion toward me. "Aren't you straight?"

"I don't know," I answered honestly. My head was spinning, my blood singing, and I felt like I didn't know anything anymore.

He sat up and faced the water, frowning. I gazed entranced at the seashell of his ear peeking from his thicket of curls. I wanted to put my lips on it. "Sorry," he said after a moment. "It's just that I promised myself after high school that I'd never get involved with another straight guy."

My heart convulsed again, and this time it was much more painful. "But, Charlie, if I like you, then I can't be straight, can I?"

He let out a soft huff of laughter that had a distinct bitter note to it. "Oh, you'd be surprised."

"Charlie," I said, hearing the desperation in my voice and hating it. "Charlie, I don't... I would never, *ever* think of you as a girl."

I knew I'd said something wrong. His shoulders stiffened, and his finely etched profile turned to stone. "Just forget it, Iowa."

Chapter Seven

When we left the rented house behind, I somehow felt almost as devastated as I had when my mother sold my childhood home. I moved back into my old dorm building, but a different room, all the way across campus from my friends, and my nights were terribly long and lonely. I dreamed of waking up and tripping downstairs to find Charlie writing at the kitchen table, LA pouring himself a bowl of sugary cereal or Cynic leaning on the railing of the balcony in his robe, smoking. We still saw each other every day, of course, but it wasn't quite the same. Whatever might've been between Charlie and me had ended with the summer. We were still friends, just as much as we'd been before summer, but no more than that. Seeing him across the table from me at the Blackbird, fully dressed, in his gold-rimmed glasses, scribbling away in a notebook, it was hard to believe that he was the same person who had drifted off to sleep beside me, half-naked, day after day. I had trouble believing that I'd actually kissed him, and sometimes I almost convinced myself that it had all been a delirious, sun-induced fever dream.

My feelings hadn't changed, though. I still felt the same swoop in my gut when I caught sight of him, the same fuzziness in my brain every time we interacted. If he'd thought I stared at him a lot before, it was nothing compared to now, and I didn't even try to hide it. I hadn't given up on Charlie. He had kissed me back on that dock, and I wouldn't forget it, the way his mouth had opened so eagerly, the tiny noise he'd made in the back of his throat. Even though he'd thought better of it afterward, his first instinct had been to kiss me back, and that had to mean something. All I could do now was hope that he would change his mind and give me a chance. Though I had indeed thought of myself as straight until very recently, there was not an ounce of doubt in my mind that I wanted to be with Charlie — not just kiss him, not just sleep with him, but *be* with him. There was also no doubt in my mind that I wanted him as a man, as my boyfriend, though I had no idea how to convince him that part was true.

Shortly after the semester started, LA and Lindsay got back together with alarming suddenness. They both claimed that they had needed a summer apart to realize they were better off together. Cynic disapproved and refused to welcome her back into the group, but I couldn't begrudge the two of them happiness when I'd so recently gotten my own taste of what heartbreak felt like. Once, when we sat in our booth at the Blackbird, LA and Lindsay on one side, Charlie and me on the other (Cynic was off sulking), Lindsay informed me that one of her friends found me attractive and had asked for my phone number. I replied that I was flattered but wasn't interested because I already had my eye on someone. LA demanded to know who, but I wouldn't tell him, and Charlie buried his face in a book, cheeks turning ruddy.

It did occur to me more than once to let LA in on my secret. I was dying to tell someone, and sometimes I felt so pent up with bottled emotions I feared I would scream it aloud in class. LA was my best friend, and he was sympathetic, compassionate and now experienced in the realm of romantic woes. However, I was uncertain about his ability to keep his cool after learning such juicy information, and I worried he would do or say something to mortify Charlie and drive him even further away from me. It also occurred to me to take my troubles to Mara and Valerie. They didn't know Charlie particularly well, which might make things easier. Perhaps they could even give me some advice on the matter of Charlie's concerns about my sexuality. But in the end, though I never would have seen it coming, the person I told was Cynic.

He was working on some new compositions and spending a lot of time in the practice rooms again. Sometimes I joined him to listen and give him my inexpert opinions, which he claimed was helpful to his process. One day, we were sitting on the piano bench together while he tried to teach me *Chopsticks*. I would have expected Cynic to be an impatient teacher, but he actually wasn't. He was mild and good-tempered, and he didn't laugh at me no matter how many times I messed up. Cynic was always softer in the presence of a piano. There was an air of camaraderie and intimacy between us that I had experienced with Charlie and LA but not with Cynic—he had a way of keeping me on edge most of the time. And somehow, without making the conscious decision to, I ended up telling him what had happened that summer.

He sat back and appraised me as though he'd never seen me before, one eyebrow arched. "You like Charlie? Damn, Iowa. I always thought you were straight."

"That's what Charlie thinks too." I sighed.

"Well, did you tell him you're not?"

I shook my head. "I told him I don't know. And I really don't know, Cyn. I've never exactly put it to the test."

He considered this, inscrutable thoughts flickering behind his dark eyes. "So should we?"

"What?" I asked stupidly.

Instead of answering, he reached around to grasp me by the back of the neck, the same as I'd done to Charlie, then he was kissing me. He was an excellent kisser, of course. I'd seen him kiss dozens of people and had always thought it looked like he knew what he was doing. I kissed him back, at first because I didn't know what else to do, then because I was enjoying it. I didn't feel what I'd felt with Charlie — that cardiac burst in my chest — but there was something else, a slower and subtler feeling that started out small, then grew.

He broke away abruptly, leaving me dazed and breathless, and remarked. "Well, you're a good kisser, but that doesn't really tell me if you're straight or not." With that, he stood up and stepped over the piano bench. "Shall we go to the Blackbird? I could use a drink."

I hesitated, realizing to my dismay that it wouldn't exactly be a good idea for me to stand up right now. He looked back at me over his shoulder, and a slow smirk spread across his face. "Oh, Iowa," he said in the sweet, playful tone he'd used to welcome me home after work each day. "Honey, you're not straight."

Before he could leave, I called after him in a moment of panic, "Cyn, don't tell Charlie about this."

He laughed. "Well, you'd better tell him then. Don't you want him to know you're not straight?"

I had no desire to tell Charlie that I'd made out with his best friend, but I was more afraid that Cynic would tell him and it would appear that I'd been hiding it. So I waited for a chance to get him alone, which wasn't easy because he'd gone back to his old methods of avoiding being alone with me. Finally, I caught him after hours in a study room at the library where I'd discovered he hid away sometimes when he had something serious to work on. He gave me a wary look when I slipped in and shut the door as if he thought I might be there to make a move on him.

"I have to tell you something," I said, sitting down across the table from him.

He eyed me uneasily. "All right."

"Cynic kissed me."

"Oh," he said with a dismissive air. "Yeah, that sounds like Cynic."

I watched in astonishment as he returned to his work. "What do you mean, that sounds like Cynic?" When he didn't answer, I pressed, "Have you and him ever...?"

He shot me a look, the bright screen of his laptop reflected in his glasses. "Have we what?"

"You know," I insisted, unable to voice it out loud.

His eyes flicked downward again. "I don't see how that's any of your business."

"You have," I exclaimed, unsure why I was so surprised. Hadn't I suspected so from the beginning?

"Charlie, why aren't you dating Cynic? He's your best friend. You love each other. You're practically in a relationship already. Sure, he sleeps around, but he'd stop for you — I know he would." I was certain of it all of a sudden, certain that Cynic would give up his wayward lifestyle in a heartbeat if Charlie asked him to. He would have to be crazy not to.

Charlie was now looking at me incredulously. "Do you want me to date Cynic?"

"No," I said, a bit too loudly for the library. I reminded myself that the study rooms weren't soundproof. "I don't want you to date Cynic. I just want to understand why. He's gorgeous, he's talented, he's brilliant... He's a dick, but he's also an incredibly good person, so why — "

"Iowa," he interrupted me with a smile pulling at the corner of his mouth. "Are you sure *you're* not the one who's in love with Cynic?"

I made a face. "I just need to know why, Charlie."

"Fine," he sighed, sitting back in his chair. "We hooked up a few times freshman year when we were roommates. You try sharing a room with Cynic without sleeping with him. It wasn't anything serious, and we don't do it anymore. Cynic and I would never work as a couple — we're better off as friends."

I was speechless for a second. Truthfully, the idea of the two of them together excited me almost as much as it upset me. "But *why*?" I asked.

He grimaced. "Look, Cynic needs me, okay? He doesn't need another fuck buddy. He needs someone he can count on. If we dated, we would definitely break up, but as friends we can stay together forever. I seriously don't think he could live without me."

I nodded. My chest was starting to hurt again. I understood now that Charlie loved Cynic in a way that he would never love me. In fact, in all likelihood, Cynic was the love of his life.

He studied me for a long moment, then let out a sigh of resignation. "Okay," he said. "We can go on one date."

"You and Cynic?" I asked, confused.

He ducked his head to hide a smile. "Me and you, idiot."

I'd never been so nervous for a date before. I had no idea what we should do. Taking him to a restaurant or a movie seemed too ordinary, and taking him to a performance at the theater was too much in line with our everyday lives and wouldn't feel like a date at all. I honestly didn't want to go anywhere public with him, not because I was self-conscious but because I wanted him all to myself the way it had been on the lakeshore that summer. If I'd had my way, we wouldn't have gone on a date at all but simply back to my room to listen to music or talk about books or... But I certainly didn't want to give him the impression that all I wanted out of this was sex. I was petrified that I was going to do something wrong and scare him away again. Now that I had my chance, I was determined not to blow it.

I ended up blowing off class that Friday and driving around until I found a picturesque and quiet park with a sunny, secluded hilltop overlooking Lake Michigan. It was late September but still very warm and the weather had promised to remain warm the following day, though there was a small chance of rain. I went to the most expensive grocery store in town and bought pretentious food that I couldn't afford — though I knew Charlie didn't care in the slightest about things like that—and a pricey bottle of champagne. I probably could have enlisted Cynic's help—he knew so much more about these things—but I felt somewhat awkward around him after our tête-à-tête in the practice room (particularly after the impact it had had on me).

I was strangely shy when I picked Charlie up at his dorm the following afternoon, embarrassed about my car, the crack in the windshield and the fact that the AC didn't work. But he didn't seem to mind. He turned on the radio and rolled down the window, tanned arm resting on the windowsill, hair whipping around his face as we drove. He was wearing the sunglasses he'd worn by the lake all summer and the same powder-blue button-down shirt I'd told him to take off that stiflingly hot day when he'd dunked me underwater. Summer Charlie was back, I realized, and my shyness melted after that. I couldn't stop looking at him, which was ill-advised because I was driving, and he kept rolling his eyes at me and smiling.

I worried that someone would have taken the spot I'd picked out on the hill, but there was no one around when we arrived. I also worried that the fluffy white clouds gathering overhead would thicken and turn to rain, but they didn't. They passed over the sun, throwing dramatic shadows, then scudded along on their way, letting the brilliant sunlight stream down to glitter on the surface of the lake. We sat in the grass— after all my preparation, I'd still managed to forget a blanket—and picked at the fancy food I'd bought. Neither of us were able to eat much. My stomach was fluttering, and I could barely taste the cheese and crackers and smoked salmon. We did, however, quickly drink all of the champagne. I can't even recall what we talked about—my brain was so fuzzy with endorphins. But at some point we lapsed into a tense, potent silence, sitting side by side, his knee touching mine.

I glanced over and saw that he was biting his lip, and it dawned on me that he was just as nervous as I was. He met my gaze. His sunglasses were pushed up on his head so I could see every green fleck in his eyes. Then, all at once, we were kissing again. I wound up on top of him, pushing him into the grass, my tongue in his mouth, which was sweet with the heady taste of champagne. He kissed me back with every ounce of eagerness as he had on the dock that day, but this time it seemed he had no reservations. I could hardly believe it. I kept thinking I was going to wake up in my dorm room, soaked in sweat, and realize that I'd been having yet another erotic dream about him. My hands found their way up under his shirt, and his skin shivered under my fingertips, diaphragm expanding and contracting as he sucked down air. Scarcely thinking, I started fumbling with the button of his shorts, then he broke away, panting. "Jesus, Iowa, slow down."

"Why?" I asked, grinning, though I knew I'd gone too far for the public setting.

His lips were curved too, damp and slightly swollen from my attack. "Well, for one thing, this is a public park—we could be arrested. For another thing, I didn't bring any protection. And for a third thing, this is our first date."

"Is it?" I inquired. I'd begun to think of every day we'd spent on the dock together that summer as a date.

"Yes," he replied, trying not to smile and failing. "You didn't think I was just going to give it up immediately, did you? I still haven't made up my mind about this."

"It seems like you've made up your mind," I pointed out, indicating his supine form.

"Okay, maybe I have." He hesitated. "But the thing is, I've had trouble in the past with cis guys like you who think they know what they're doing but then just end up treating me…how they would treat a woman. Especially because I'm, well, submissive."

Hearing him say "submissive" made me want to pin him down again and bite his lower lip until he squirmed. But I withheld the urge. "I understand, Charlie."

"You might think you do, but I think you probably don't. So let's just take it slow, okay?"

"Okay."

However, it soon became clear that taking it slow was going to be exceedingly difficult. We made out again in the car outside his dorm, even though there were plenty of people walking past, and I mumbled in his ear, "Invite me in."

"You sound like a vampire," he snickered.

"Come on, Charlie. We don't have to go all the way."

"Forget it, Iowa." The words were so different from the last time he'd spoken them because this time he didn't mean it.

We said goodnight, and I went home to relieve my urges myself, hoping that Charlie was doing the same thing.

.

Chapter Eight

I would have thought Charlie to be the type of boyfriend who was squeamish about public displays of affection, but I was pleased to find that he wasn't. LA was gobsmacked when we casually informed him at the café that we were now dating, my arm draped around Charlie's shoulders.

Lindsay shook her head at his shock and said, "You really didn't see that coming? Didn't you see how red Charlie's face was when Iowa told us that he liked someone?" LA got onboard after that and started planning copious cheesy double dates while the rest of us exchanged glances and cringed. Cynic seemed fine with the development at first—he really did. Since his unorthodox measures had actually helped Charlie and me get together, I'd gotten over the incident in the practice room. He was conspicuously absent from the café more often, but I chalked that up to his distaste for Lindsay.

I'd never been in a relationship I was so proud to put on display. I took great pleasure in the glances we got when we crossed campus holding hands or kissed before heading off to class. I wanted everyone to know that I was dating Charlie St. James, and I hoped that people talked about us even if they said homophobic things. I'd fully embraced my new identity as a non-straight man — though I still didn't know what label I fell under — and I liked the way it changed how people treated me. I felt that my opinion was sometimes taken more seriously in class now that I was no longer speaking from a place of straight, white male privilege. The acquaintances I'd met through Mara and Valerie now treated me as one of their own, including me in their ongoing banter about being queer. When I met someone new, I tried to mention my boyfriend as early as possible so they knew where to categorize me.

Of course, I still had a lot to learn about being a member of the queer community. One thing I had to keep in mind was that I was still extremely privileged. I hadn't had to deal with homophobic abuse growing up or face coming out my family — if and when I ever told my mother, I doubted she would care. I hadn't had to fight for marriage equality or the right to hold my boyfriend's hand in public. All the rights I had now had been earned for me by people who fought, bled, and often died — mostly trans women of color, Valerie frequently reminded me. I had a lot of history to catch up on, including events that had taken place within my lifetime that I had missed. My queer friends were happy to educate me, though they did tease me sometimes, and Charlie was eternally patient. He thought it was cute, he claimed.

He was always calling me "cute," and I joked that perhaps he meant "ruggedly handsome." He snorted at me and said, "No, I mean cute." Apparently he'd always thought so, ever since he'd first noticed me, which was the time LA had called me onstage to ask my opinion about his Japanese accent. This amazed me.

"Even when you thought I was a bigot?" I asked.

"Yes," he replied. "I thought you were an adorable bigot."

His affection for me was an unending source of wonder and disbelief. Whenever I didn't see him for a few hours, I would start to think I'd made it all up. Then when I saw him again and he snatched my hand or stood on his toes to kiss me, the cycle started all over again. I couldn't fathom my own luck. I walked around in a daze, waiting for the delusion to shatter and continuously awestruck when it didn't.

In the end, we failed in our attempt to take it slow. We barely lasted more than a week. After our second official date, which went much the same as the first one except that we were in a movie theater, I pressed him up against the front door of his dorm building and kissed him until he mumbled, "Fuck. You'd better come in." In his dorm room, we fumbled our way to the bed in the dark and undressed each other clumsily. He told me there were condoms in the bedside drawer, and I knocked the lamp over trying to find them. He laughed while I muttered, "Shit, shit, shit." Once I'd gotten myself sorted out, I crawled back over to him. He looked up at me, his face featureless in the dark.

"Are you sure you want to do this?" I asked, suddenly shy.

"Yeah," he breathed. His breath was minty from the nicotine gum he'd started using — he hadn't smoked a cigarette since I'd told him about my father. "Just go easy on me, okay? It's been a while."

It had been a while for me too — since my drunken one-night stand in California and this was so, so different. I recalled what he'd said about cis men treating him like a woman and became afraid that I was about to make the same mistake. "How do you like it?" I asked him hesitantly.

He reached up and put his arms around my neck. "I'll show you," he whispered, pulling me down on top of him.

* * * *

Afterward, I lay blissfully exhausted with my arm wrapped around him, my face buried in his soft curls. Out of nowhere, he started shaking with silent laughter.

"Hey," I grumbled. "What the hell are you laughing at?"

He laughed harder for a minute, then managed to answer, "Sorry. I just never thought I'd hear myself moaning the word 'Iowa' while getting fucked."

I had to laugh a little then too. "Next time, you can call me 'Will'."

He went quiet, then murmured, "Okay."

The sex was better than I could've imagined. Seeing him in public drove me crazy now, and I constantly whispered in his ear and grabbed his ass when I thought no one was looking. I couldn't wait to get him back to his dorm room or mine at the end of the day to worship him in the dark for a few hours. Pretty soon, we rarely spent a night apart. Everything else escalated rapidly too. Scarcely a month had gone by before I mumbled into his ear one night that I loved him.

"Fuck, Will," he replied. "Don't just say that." At first, he only called me by my name in the bedroom, but soon enough it was all the time.

"I'm not just saying it," I told him. It was true. Sure, we'd only been dating for a month, but I had loved him for longer than that. In fact, I'd loved him even before that summer, though I hadn't realized it at the time. It was impossible to identify the moment I'd started loving him, but I'd begun to suspect that it had been ridiculously early in our relationship, before we were even friends, before he would even make eye contact with me. I didn't tell him this because I thought it might scare him — truthfully, it scared me too.

He didn't say it back that time, but somehow that didn't perturb me. I knew he would say it when he was ready. And I didn't have to wait that long. It was only a week or two before he shyly told me that he loved me too. I didn't have any trouble believing him. Now that we were sleeping together, my doubts had dissipated like the fleeting frost that covered the sidewalks in the mornings. It was obvious that he loved me, and I no longer bothered to ask myself why. The reason didn't matter as long as he kept inexplicably doing so.

On weekends, we often lay in bed together reading, as I'd wanted to from the beginning instead of forcing ourselves to go on dates. But sometimes Charlie would write, tapping away on his laptop, the white page and lines of mysterious black text reflected in his glasses. He was fussy about sharing his writing with me, insisting that it wasn't finished or that he still had some editing to do. Once, when I'd pestered him enough, he divulged that he was writing a play — a musical, actually.

"Am I in it?" I asked, nudging him with my foot.

He made a face and said, "No. I do, in fact, have interests other than you."

He told me it was about Amelio Robles Ávila, a colonel in the Mexican Revolution who had lived openly as a transgender man. He had been known to draw a pistol on anyone who'd called him "Doña," which Charlie mimed with one hand, making me smile. One of the reasons he admired Robles was because he lived to the age of ninety-five, which was more or less unheard of for trans people of the time period. Even today, trans people had significantly shorter average lifespans than cis people, due to murder and suicide. This was news to me, and I was unsettled by the matter-of-fact way he stated it.

"For once, a trans person got a happy ending," he said. "I think that's an important story to tell. Kids need to know that. You know, the first time I learned trans men existed was when I saw *Boys Don't Cry*. Can you imagine how that messed me up?"

I admitted I'd never seen it, and he advised me not to watch it.

"Robles was a badass," he told me, "and trans kids need badass role models—not just bleak warnings of how their lives might end...although those stories are important too."

"Can I read it?" I asked him.

He bit his lip, then answered, "It's not finished, but I guess you can read the first act if you really want to."

It was brilliant, of course. I wouldn't have expected any less of him. I particularly liked the songs, although I couldn't read music so I didn't know how they were supposed to sound. After some coaxing, he grabbed the acoustic guitar that leaned against the foot of his bed and showed me. It was incredible. Parts of the songs were in Spanish—he spoke quite a bit of Spanish and Portuguese, both of which I found insanely sexy. When he asked me what I thought at the end, I just grabbed him and kissed him until he laughed breathlessly. I was certain at that moment that no one had ever been more in love than I was.

It bothered me what he'd said about trans people's shortened lifespans. Valerie had become very important to me, my almost-roommate Riley had become a good friend too, and several other trans people had taken on significant roles in my life. It was fascinating how knowing one of them connected me to them all. Riley called it "the trans hive mind." I couldn't bear it if anything were to happen to any of them. I did watch *Boys Don't Cry*, against Charlie's advice, and bawled my eyes out. For a time, Charlie took on the fragility in my mind again that he had when I'd thought he had a terminal illness. This was magnified tenfold when he confided to me that he'd been suicidal his freshman year, had planned a dozen ways to take his own life and had even written notes.

I knew that Charlie had saved Cynic's life that year when he'd found him passed out drunk in a snowbank, but I didn't know that Cynic had also saved Charlie's. "He just needed me so much," Charlie explained. "I couldn't leave him alone." He talked to me often of Cynic, though he steered around the romantic or sexual parts of their relationship.

"You know, when I first got here, I was terrified about having a male roommate," he told me once. "Especially when I met him and found out he was six-foot-two, twenty-three years old and filthy rich. I thought I was going to get fucking murdered. I didn't want to sneak around and live in fear that he was going to find out about me, so on the first night I sat him down and told him I was trans and that if he wanted a different roommate I completely understood and I would put in a request to change rooms in the morning."

"What did he say?" I prompted.

"He sat there and stared at me for the longest time — he was baked out of his mind, by the way. Then he said, 'Well, thank God. At least I never have to worry about whether your dick is bigger than mine'."

While I was relieved and grateful that Cynic had kept Charlie in this world, I couldn't help but be jealous too. I had always admired Cynic, somewhat envied him and been unwittingly attracted to him, I now realized. But now, hearing about his history with Charlie and seeing the way Charlie's face lit up when he talked about him was nothing short of agonizing. It was hard to bite back the acidic remarks that rose my tongue sometimes when Charlie relayed some miraculous thing Cynic had said or done, or spouted about one of the many spectacular trips they'd taken. I was bitterly conscious of my inability to take Charlie on trips, or even buy him dinner, or to blow his mind with my artistic genius. Cynic's superiority to me seemed infinite at times, and it made my gut ache, especially because every time I saw Cynic I found that I still adored him as much as ever.

Cynic had finally eased up on Lindsay, and the five of us hung out together again, crowded into our booth at the Blackbird. Charlie and I had started working on grad school applications, and we talked about it a great deal. We were focusing on the East Coast, particularly New York. He was aiming for the Ivy League, while I had my sights set lower, but I hoped to stay as close to him as possible. My academic performance at Weston had been fairly impressive, and I thought I had a good chance of earning some hefty scholarships. LA and Lindsay were also set on moving to New York and were desperate to impress the talent scouts who would appear at Weston's theater productions later in the year. Cynic had no specific plans for the future beyond graduating, which he still claimed he was only doing to stick it to his father. Of course, Cynic would never have to work a day in his life. He could flit around the world, drinking and debauching until it killed him if he wanted to, though I thought it would be a terrible waste. He didn't belong in academia — that was clear — but he certainly belonged on a stage somewhere.

He'd begun to construct his plans for the future around ours. His mother hardly ever used her apartment in Manhattan anymore, and she'd been thinking of selling it, but he thought he could talk her into keeping it if we put it to use. We wouldn't even have to pay rent. The rest of us were so overawed by this idea, we couldn't bring ourselves to put any stock in it. It was too good to be true — it was the stuff of sitcoms, a free luxury apartment in New York. I'd been so happy there with Charlie, LA and Cynic over spring break, and so happy with them in the rented house over the summer, I couldn't resist fantasizing about it. I pictured Charlie and me studying in that marvelous library in the evenings, LA and Lindsay running lines at the gleaming dining room table, and Cynic at the piano, cigarette hanging from his lip, his whiskey glass leaving a ring on the invaluable wood that Charlie or I would anxiously scrub at later. Yet the idea of being utterly dependent on Cynic was also repugnant to me. I had a horrifying vision of walking in to find him and

Charlie together on the piano bench, as I'd found them so many times in the practice rooms, except this time they were kissing, and I wouldn't be able to do a thing about it because I lived at Cynic's expense.

Chapter Nine

If there was a turning point, it was that winter break, when Cynic insisted we were going to Europe and wouldn't take no for an answer. LA and Lindsay were going to California and I'd hoped we might join them. I'd had such a good time there the previous year. But Charlie wanted to go to Europe, and I wanted to be with him. We would go to Spain and Portugal, where we would rely on Charlie's linguistic abilities, then France, where we would rely on Cynic's. Once I'd resigned myself to the idea, I was excited. I'd never been overseas and had thought I might never have the chance to go. On the interminable flight, Charlie slept on my shoulder and we shared earbuds to listen to music, while Cynic sat on his other side, drinking and flirting with the flight attendants, fingers tapping as though they itched to hold a cigarette.

It was a life-changing trip. I could scarcely comprehend that those cobblestone streets and bright stucco buildings existed under the same sky as my hometown. Barcelona and Lisbon in the winter were breathtaking, melancholy and wildly romantic, devoid of their usual tourist throngs. The sky was pearl-gray most days, and it rained off and on, but I didn't mind in the slightest. We visited innumerable churches and museums and ate food that almost brought tears to my eyes because I realized that I'd never really tasted food before. Everywhere we went, there was an air of preservation, of changelessness, that I had never encountered in the United States, as if we'd fallen into a pocket of reality where clocks didn't exist and everything was eternal. Charlie and I held hands unabashedly, and I pulled him into doorways when it started downpouring to kiss him frantically for a few minutes before the rain let up. We tried not to display too much physical affection in front of Cynic.

It started slowly, and I thought I was imagining it at first. Cynic had always teased me, but it seemed like there was a bite to his japes now, an underlying cruelty that hadn't been there before. He knew all my weakest points, my deepest insecurities, and exactly how to prod them — my lack of money, my inferior shoes, my ignorance of other cultures and languages, my cluelessness about food and wine. When I referred to a bottle of cava as champagne, he laughed at me as though I'd mistaken night for day. He quizzed me on my knowledge of the places we visited and watched with pleasure when I flushed because I didn't know the answers. Even the way he said my name was different, drawling the word "Iowa" like he had that first time when I'd thought he was simply slurring his words. Bit by bit, he forced me back into the role I'd adopted at the beginning of my time at Weston that I'd been trying so hard to vacate ever since. In his presence at least, I once more became a caricature of myself.

That wasn't the end of it though. Charlie became the target of a different kind of abuse. Cynic said things to him in Spanish so rapidly I couldn't catch a word, but I was certain by the expression on Charlie's face that they were dirty. He didn't touch him the way he used to anymore—slinging an arm around his shoulders or tousling his hair—because he must have known I wouldn't abide it. But the looks he shot him sometimes were a thousand times worse. Cynic was so naturally seductive I could swear he'd invented eye-fucking.

Things rapidly went downhill after we arrived in Paris. I hadn't realized how fluent Cynic was in French—I'd sort of thought he was bluffing. It turned out he spoke it like a native, or that was how the Parisians acted anyway. He would lure women over to our table in bars, and I was sure by their shocked stares and nervous laughter that he was telling them vile things about me. Once, he dragged us into a gay bar and lavished attention on a stunningly attractive man all evening, and when he pulled him in for a kiss, I saw him make eye contact with Charlie over the man's shoulder.

Dark thoughts started to grow in my mind. I began to have suspicions that Charlie hadn't told me the full truth when he'd described his casual relationship with Cynic. I began to think it hadn't been just "a few times," and it hadn't ended with their freshman year. In fact, I gradually convinced myself that they had been romantically involved during their trip to South America last year. I recalled Charlie saying, *"You try sharing a room with Cynic without sleeping with him."* They had certainly shared a room during that trip and, I now concluded, a bed too. Charlie had misled me, and I wasn't angry at him for it because I knew he'd only done it because he liked me. Whatever had happened with Cynic in the past, it was unquestionable that he was mine now. But that didn't stop the envy and agony from eating away at my heart.

Charlie and I were able to escape Cynic a few times by going places he wouldn't be caught dead at—the Eiffel Tower, the Arc de Triomphe and restaurants he deemed to be tourist traps. Then we had a wonderful time, although we had to pay for things ourselves and therefore couldn't be too spontaneous. I wanted to buy him everything that drew his eye on the Champs-Élysées—leather jackets, wallets, shirts, scarves and fancy notebook paper. I wanted to take him to the most overpriced restaurants in town and tell him to order anything on the menu because money was no object. I watched the way Cynic idly passed his credit card to waiters and sales clerks, flourishing it between two fingers without a thought. I began to hate that elegant piece of black plastic. I wished he would drunkenly drop his wallet in the river and have to call his parents to beg for money.

No matter how unkind he was to me, I felt that I couldn't say anything. He'd flown me to Europe and was going to fly me back, and he paid for my meals, drinks and museum tickets just like he had in New York. Charlie had said back then that money was Cynic's love language, but now it felt like a weapon. I was afraid that if I spoke up to defend myself, he would abandon me here, and I would have no way to get home. I had nightmares about wandering the streets of Paris without a penny in my pocket, unable to communicate with anyone to ask for help. I was completely at Cynic's mercy, and he liked it that way. That was why he'd brought me here.

I finally snapped one night in our luxurious suite that overlooked the Seine. Cynic was drunk in the broody, sophisticated way only he could pull off, lounging on a velvet chaise, a glass of Merlot cradled in one hand. He looked magnificent, and he knew it, and it was infuriating. He'd bought a new shirt that day, a ludicrously expensive shirt that was the same deep burgundy color as his wine, and it complemented the rich ochre hue of his skin. The chiseled angles of his face cast sharp shadows beneath his jawline and cheekbones, and the lamplight glittered in his dark eyes, giving him the aspect of a slightly deranged king who might order my execution at any moment.

"Well, I'm bored," he remarked, swirling his wine around his glass. "What do you think, St. James? Iowa?" Then he said something in French that I didn't understand except for the distinct words *"ménage à trois."*

Charlie winced and looked at me. We knew why he was making this suggestion. We'd refrained from having sex the entire trip so far, out of fear that Cynic would hear us, but last night we'd made what we'd thought to be a very quiet exception.

"That's enough," I told Cynic sharply. "Don't you get it? Charlie and I are dating—not just fucking around. I know that's a difficult concept for you. He's with me, he doesn't want you and neither do I."

Cynic regarded me for a long moment, sculpted face betraying nothing. I knew that with his barbed tongue he could flay the flesh from my bones if he wanted to, and I braced myself for it. But he said nothing. Instead, he got up, flung open the French doors, and stepped out onto the balcony, and for a wild, irrational instant I thought he was going to jump. But he leaned on the railing and lit a cigarette, and I tried to slow my pounding heart. After a minute, Charlie slipped past me and went out after him. I went to bed and dreamed that the two of them crept past my doorway into Cynic's room and shut the door behind them. But in the morning, Charlie was asleep next to me.

When he woke, he told me quietly, "You can't say things like that to him, okay? I know he's being an asshole, but... He's fragile."

"He's not fragile," I griped. "He's fucking spoiled. He needs to grow up and stop acting like a kid."

"Please, Will," he said. He looked so angelic in the soft white light that emanated through the curtains, hair tousled, the rumpled imprint of the bed sheet florid on his cheek. My heart melted.

"Fine," I sighed.

Cynic was civil for the rest of the trip. Either my words had subdued him or Charlie had said something more powerful—I thought the latter was more likely. He never did what I feared most—he never threatened or even joked about leaving me behind in Europe. I should have realized that Cynic wouldn't go that far. He did love me, at least a little, I've come to think, in his own peculiar way.

When the spring semester started, Cynic kept his distance from the group for a while. LA was concerned about it. He asked me more than once if something had happened in Europe, but I wouldn't tell him the details. It just didn't seem like my place. Every day at the café started to feel a bit like a double date with LA and Lindsay running lines for their spring auditions and gushing about the parts they hoped to play, and Charlie and me finishing up and sending out the last of our grad school applications. I found myself warming more toward Lindsay, who I'd never disliked but had never felt close to either. She'd had a more difficult time last year than I'd realized. Her brother had died of an opioid overdose in April, she told us, and she'd asked LA to keep it quiet at the time. It had been a large factor in their relationship troubles and temporary break-up—she'd been horribly depressed and had almost dropped out of Weston.

She—I could tell—was relieved at Cynic's absence. She confessed to me privately that he'd always set her on edge. "LA's so excited about the apartment in New York," she said, picking at her chipped nail polish. "But I just don't know if I could do it, you know? I don't know if I could live under his thumb like that."

It unsettled me somewhat that she'd chosen to disclose this to me. Was it that obvious that I felt the same? Was the tension between Cynic and me that palpable? Was he even my friend? Even as I had these doubts, though, I had to acknowledge that I missed Cynic terribly—not the Cynic I'd known in Europe, of course, but the one I'd known before. I missed his wisecracks, his gentle teasing, his pretentious remarks and his subtle but steadfast compassion for his friends. I felt badly about telling him off in Paris, even though he'd had it coming, and I wanted to make things right with him. I just didn't know how.

I finally got the chance a few weeks into the semester. It was LA's twenty-second birthday party, which made me feel ancient. I would be twenty-seven in April, as would Cynic—we'd actually been born only eight days apart. He came to the party—LA would've been devastated if he hadn't—but he wasn't his usual spotlight-seeking self. He kept to the sidelines and left the piano in the common room for a far less talented junior to play. Charlie was there for a few hours, but then he left, claiming to have a headache, but I presumed he just wanted to work on his musical. He never seemed to enjoy parties much, though we attended them frequently. I would have liked to go with him, but I stayed because LA seemed disappointed that he was leaving. I played a drinking game consisting of embarrassing theater exercises with Lindsay and some of her friends. I was slightly tipsy by the time I spotted Cynic stalking out the back door and made up my mind to follow him.

It was snowing outside, and my breath puffed out in a white cloud as if I were a smoker. Cynic was actually smoking, of course, leaning against the wall under the security light. His tight, cropped curls were dusted with snowflakes, and he wore his black wool greatcoat with the collar flipped up. I wasn't dressed warmly enough so I folded my arms across my chest as I joined him.

We said nothing for a minute. Then he exhaled a stream of white smoke and said, "Sorry." He didn't have to specify what for. "I would try to blame it on the drinking, but I'm drunk right now so I guess I couldn't get away with that, huh?"

It occurred to me that this could be an opportunity to say something about his drinking, which I'd always kind of wanted to. But I felt perhaps it wasn't the right moment. I also felt like a hypocrite because I drank too, much more than I had before coming to Weston, though Cynic had admittedly played a large role in that. Instead, I just asked him, "Are you okay?"

I thought this might earn me some flippant remark, but he paused thoughtfully. "I know what it looks like," he began at last, "but I swear I'm not in love with

Charlie. I'm happy for you two, really. It's just sort of hard when your best friend starts dating someone, you know? And it seems like LA's sticking with Lindsay now... I guess I feel like a bit of a fifth wheel."

I felt an almost painful twinge of fondness for him at that moment. "Yeah, but you're the steering wheel, Cyn. Without you, we'd go off the road."

He smirked at my lame joke, but I meant it. LA had befriended me first, but Cynic was the one who had invited me to the Blackbird. He was the one who had welcomed me into the group. Without Cynic, none of the amazing things that had happened in these past two years would have happened. Perhaps that was what I admired about him the most—he made things happen.

After a time, he said, "I was thinking I've had enough adventures for a while. Maybe I'll go home to Boston for spring break and rub my graduation in my father's face. Give you and Charlie some time alone."

I'd almost forgotten that he'd grown up in Boston, which was funny because his accent was so pronounced. "I applied to Boston University," I told him.

He glanced at me sidelong. "Really? I thought you were aiming for New York."

"Well, NYU is still my first choice, but I've got to keep my options open. And Boston isn't too far from New York."

"Hmm. I got kicked out of BU, you know. It was the first college I tried. But I'm sure you would have more success."

"I'm really glad you're graduating, Cyn," I said.

"Yeah." He chuckled. "It's good to finish at least one thing in your life."

Chapter Ten

Cynic was around more after that, but I'm not sure he was ever fully himself again. I'm also not sure I ever truly believed that he wasn't in love with Charlie. I might have been biased, but I couldn't fathom how someone could know Charlie so intimately, could go to bed with him, without falling in love with him. I knew Cynic wasn't as sentimental as I was, but he wasn't heartless either. He returned to the practice rooms to prepare for the annual concert in March, but I didn't drop in on him as much as I used to, and Charlie didn't either. I made a point of not prying into their friendship, but I got the sense that they weren't as close anymore. Charlie didn't talk to me about him as often, and when he did, his face didn't light up the same way.

I'd landed myself another tutoring job, this time at the local high school, and that kept me busy for a few hours after class each day. I enjoyed it even more than working with the middle school students and had begun to think that teaching adults might be even more fun. I'd never envisioned myself spending my whole life in the academic realm, but now I looked at my professors with new eyes, wondering how hard they worked, how tired they were, how many papers they had to grade in the evenings and whether it was worth it. Charlie thought it was a wonderful idea and joked that at least I could bring in a stable income then, while he committed to the life of a starving artist. My insides turned warm whenever he alluded to us spending our lives together, even if he was joking around.

I was more anxious about my grad school applications than I let on, worried that I wouldn't get into any schools in New York. I was sure Charlie would be accepted into his top choice, Columbia, though he had his doubts. I told myself that even if I had to go somewhere two or three hours away, we could still make it work. I would drive to see him every weekend. But I'd heard such dreadful things about long-distance relationships, I couldn't stop myself from fretting over it.

When he got his response from Columbia, he made me open it for him while he sat with his face in his hands, though I could already tell by the thickness of the envelope that it was an acceptance letter. He didn't stop smiling for a whole day and even called his mother, who I'd never heard him talk to before. I heard her voice rise in excitement on the other end, and they lapsed between English and Portuguese throughout the call. A couple days later, I got two envelopes in my mailbox — a thin one from NYU and a thick one from Boston University. I was disappointed but also thrilled. The acceptance letter from BU was even more beautiful than my acceptance letter to Weston, which I still had tucked away in a drawer.

We went to Cynic's concert in March, and his performance was even more tremendous and transfixing than the previous year's. Again I felt that bizarre paralysis, that leaden weight in my limbs while he played. Charlie watched with the same entranced expression that had made me think he was in love with Cynic last year, and I had the same intrusive thought now. But truthfully, I think everyone in the concert hall was a little bit in love with Cynic that night, including me. His parents again failed to make an appearance, but he assured me they would be at graduation if only to make sure he wasn't lying about it.

Shortly afterward, LA landed himself the role of a lifetime — he would be playing Hamlet. His destiny was more or less decided then, as he and Lindsay reminded each other constantly. He would almost certainly be discovered by a talent scout and signed to an agency before the year was out. Somehow, everything became very real for all of us then. Our time at Weston was drawing to a close, and the next chapter of our lives was opening.

I didn't get into any schools in New York, but I couldn't bring myself to suffer over it. Boston University had taken on a luminescence in my mind. I researched their English program, growing more exhilarated by the day. I even suggested that Charlie and I go with Cynic to Boston for spring break so I could see the campus. I'd forgiven him for the catastrophe in Europe.

Cynic's mother sold her apartment after all, much to Lindsay's relief and — though I would never voice it aloud — mine. I couldn't bear the thought of Charlie living there without me, playing house with Cynic the way they had last summer, dancing around each other in the kitchen, leaving each other notes on the fridge. I was much more comfortable imagining him snug in a dorm room at Columbia, clacking away on his laptop while raindrops pattered on the window, with a tiny single bed that we would have to squeeze into when I came to visit him on weekends.

LA and Lindsay started saving to put a deposit down on an apartment, which made them feel very mature and domestic, though I knew both of them got monthly allowances from their family trusts. They would have no trouble making it in New York, and I was glad that they would be close to Charlie. Though it pains me to say it, I didn't give much of a thought to what Cynic was going to do now that his plans had fallen through. He always hated it when people bailed on him.

We planned our trip to Boston. He was going to show us every corner of his glamorous world, and I visualized it being much like our trip to New York last year rather than our trip to Europe. He bought Charlie's and my plane tickets and forwarded them to my email for some reason. I'm still not sure why, and it bothers me to this day. He probably just wanted us to know what times our flights were, but he usually took sole responsibility for that knowledge and simply told us to pack our bags. I try not to think anything of it. I really do believe that Cynic had every intention of going to Boston with us.

He turned twenty-seven the week before spring break, and we threw a party that was both his and mine because our birthdays were so close together. It was just like the old days—he played the piano while people thronged around him, singing along uproariously to *Piano Man* and other renowned classics, until Cynic got drunk and switched to his beloved 'white girl music'. To the backdrop of Adele, Taylor Swift and Lana Del Rey, Charlie and I talked with our friends, my arm draped possessively around his shoulders. We talked about Columbia and Boston University and our friends' plans for after graduation. Mara and Valerie were moving to Portland, where Mara had gotten an artist's residency. They invited Charlie and me to come visit that summer once they were settled in, and we both must've recalled Cynic's comment about beards, craft beer and camping because we exchanged a glance and grinned.

LA was chattering about *Hamlet*, as he usually was those days. Opening night would be the Friday following spring break. I could hear him bellowing, "To be, or not to be," across the room. Lindsay was quiet—I gathered that it had been almost a year since her brother had died. When she decided to leave early, I offered to walk her across campus. I had volunteered to tutor a student in the morning who was struggling with an English assignment. It wasn't my actual birthday, after all—not for another week. I was somewhat apprehensive about turning twenty-seven, especially since Charlie was still twenty-three. But seeing the way Cynic embraced it wholeheartedly made me feel a bit better.

Lindsay kissed LA goodnight, and I kissed Charlie. He normally wouldn't stay at a party so late, but this was Cynic's party. I think he was enjoying seeing his best friend back in his element for the first time in a while. Lindsay and I left and crossed campus in relative silence, our shadows stretching long and thin in the orange light of the lamp posts. I asked her if she was okay at some point, and she nodded.

"It's just weird," she said, "thinking that this time last year, everything was perfectly normal. It's crazy how a phone call in the middle of the night can flip the whole world upside down."

I said I understood, but I really didn't. My father's death hadn't come out of nowhere. It had been so excruciatingly slow it had almost come as a relief. I said goodnight to Lindsay at her dorm and watched until she was inside. The campus was safe, but she was so small my cis male ego convinced me that she needed my protection. Then I walked back to my dorm with the sense of unease that talking about sudden death always evokes. I almost considered going back to the party just to ensure Charlie got home safely. But Charlie was among friends, he could take care of himself, and he didn't need his boyfriend hovering at his shoulder every minute. That was what I told myself as I went to bed and drifted into a restive sleep.

The sound of my phone vibrating dragged me back into semi-consciousness. I couldn't find it at first and had to fumble around in my sheets. The screen was so bright it hurt my eyes, and I squinted at it with blurred vision. It was two in the morning, and LA was calling me.

"Will?" he said in a very strange, very wrong voice. As soon as I heard it, the world flipped upside down, just like Lindsay had said. "You have to come to the hospital. There's been an accident."

As I stumbled about my room, pulling on my clothes, I kept my phone glued to my ear, trying desperately to get more information out of LA. But he was even less coherent than usual, and all I could discern was that Cynic, while attempting to drive to the liquor store, had driven his car off the road. I repeatedly asked about Charlie, but he couldn't seem to understand what I was saying.

"Fuck, Will," he said, voice breaking. "They won't even let me see him."

"Charlie?" I demanded, heart pounding in my ears.

"No — Cynic."

I hung up because holding the phone to my ear was slowing me down, grabbed my keys and ran out to my car. I didn't think of Cynic even once on the drive. There was only Charlie, my Charlie, beaming down at his letter from Columbia, rolling his eyes at me when I stared at him, gazing up at me from the grass on our first date, falling asleep on the dock. I pleaded and bargained with every divine entity I'd ever heard of. I would do anything — give up grad school, become a monk, renounce all my worldly possessions and devote my life to creating sand mandalas — if only I could see him again.

When I burst into the ICU waiting room, the first thing I saw was the top of LA's sleek black hair. He was hunched over in a chair, head in his hands, sobbing brokenly. The next thing I saw was Charlie, standing there hugging himself, looking lost and bewildered but unhurt. All I could feel then was relief, even though I knew Cynic was dead, because I got to put my arms around Charlie and hold his fragile, shaking form and swear to every god I could think of that I would never let him go.

Charlie hadn't been in the car, of course. He hadn't even been aware that Cynic had left the party. LA had known, and he was a wreck over it. "He didn't seem that drunk," he kept telling me. "You know how he is. I couldn't tell."

Cynic really was dead, which I was confused about at first because LA kept referring to him in the present tense as if he might saunter out in a hospital gown at any given moment. Apparently, he had claimed that he was going to the liquor store but had actually driven out of town and wrapped his gorgeous BMW around a tree at eighty miles an hour. He had been alive, in the technical sense, until shortly before I arrived, but there had been no chance of saving him, at least not the version of him that we knew.

Charlie, however, was the one who appeared to be the victim of a traumatic brain injury. He was glassy-eyed and unresponsive, staring vacantly around him like he didn't know where he was. I wasn't even sure if he recognized me. LA wept on and off, but Charlie was dry-eyed. I couldn't seem to summon a tear either.

After he'd gathered himself a bit, LA took me aside and said, "I think you should take Charlie home. I don't think he should be here anymore."

I agreed. LA said he was staying to wait for Cynic's parents who were on their way. Irrationally, I thought to myself that they wouldn't show up, that they would miss this performance like they had missed all the others. I didn't know why, but I couldn't stop thinking of it as a performance, an elaborate end-of-the-year stunt. I told LA to text me when he was ready to leave and I would come back for him. He and Charlie had taken an Uber here when they got the call (Charlie was Cynic's emergency contact). I asked why they hadn't thought to call me right away, and LA mumbled, "I don't know. I'm sorry. We were drunk."

I took Charlie home, leading him by the hand to the car and buckling his seatbelt like he was a little kid. He didn't say a word the whole drive. Back in his dorm room, he sat on the bed and rifled through his bedside drawer for the sleeping pills he used at night sometimes. I watched him shake two into his hand.

"You shouldn't take those," I told him, having déjà vu of the time I'd told him not to smoke. "You've been drinking."

He ignored me and popped them in his mouth. Then he crawled under the covers and curled up, facing away from me. I sat on the floor by his bed, watching the slight rise and fall of his shoulders and listening to the soft sound of his breaths. It was starting to get light outside when LA texted me. I got up stiffly and grabbed the bottle of pills from the nightstand before I left.

Back at the hospital, I took the elevator up to the ICU, but LA wasn't in the waiting room. I got back in the elevator with two police officers in uniform, guns on their hips, drinking coffee out of Styrofoam cups. They were mid-conversation when I stepped in, and I realized after a second that they were talking about Cynic.

"Poor bastard," one of them, a ruddy-faced middle-aged white man, was saying. "You know, I saw this kind of shit all the time working traffic down in Detroit. They bitch about getting pulled over a lot, but what do they expect when they drive like morons?"

The other one, a younger white man, looked somewhat uncomfortable and made a small gesture in my direction. The first cop glanced over, saw me staring and shut his mouth. When the doors opened to the lobby, LA was waiting on the other side. The cops walked past him, but I stayed frozen in the elevator.

"Will?" he asked. "What's wrong?"

I kept staring after the cops, unable to answer.

He looked over his shoulder. "What? Did those guys say something to you?"

I said nothing. The elevator doors tried to close, and he blocked them with his arm.

"Come on," he said, taking my arm gently. "Let's get out of here."

He led me to the car, as I'd led Charlie only hours ago, took the keys from me and got in the driver's seat. "Don't worry, I'm sober as hell now," he told me.

I'd never ridden in the passenger seat of my own car. The crack in the windshield looked worse from this angle. He drove in silence, while I leaned my head against the window, watching the gray world rush by. About halfway home, I suddenly started banging my head against the glass, hard enough that I saw stars. LA cried, "What the fuck, Will? Stop!" and swerved as he tried to grab me. My life flashed before my eyes, not my glorious, dreamlike life from the past two years, but my bleak, tiny life in Iowa—the general store, the hospital bed in my parents' room, the 'for sale' sign that popped up in our front yard one day like an ugly, unexpected flower. I wondered if Cynic had seen his life too in that final, terrible instant and what it had looked like.

"Jesus," LA exclaimed as he righted the car. "Are you trying to make me crash? Do you know how fucking ironic that would be right now?"

I couldn't answer because I was crying too hard.

"Oh my God," he said then. "Will, please don't cry. Please, I just stopped crying, and I really don't want to start again. Look, fuck those cops, okay? Whatever they said, they don't know what they're talking about."

I couldn't tell him that I wasn't crying about what the cop had said. I was crying about my first day working at the general store when I was eighteen, when my boss had told me not to accept checks from Black people, and I had said nothing because I was poor and my father had cancer and I desperately needed the job.

Chapter Eleven

We did end up using the tickets to Boston that Cynic had bought us—to attend his funeral. The funeral home, compared to the cheap roadside establishment where I'd said farewell to my father's closed casket, was almost grotesquely grand. His casket, also closed, was every bit as elegant and imposing as he deserved. I knew he wasn't actually in there—he'd been cremated. Otherwise, the environment didn't suit him at all. The flowers were tacky, the conversation hushed and restrained, and the organ music soulless. The most absurd thing was the way his family was divided perfectly down the middle, Black on one side, white on the other. His mother sat in the front row of the Black side, looking as handsome and distinguished as I remembered in a navy-blue pantsuit and dangerously high heels. His father, a startlingly plain suburban-looking man, sat on the white side with his blond wife and robotic blond step-children.

The picture of him they had chosen to display could have been taken straight from *GQ* magazine. He gazed down on us haughtily, the suggestion of a smirk pulling at the corner of his shapely mouth as if he were about to laugh at us. His mother gave a very composed and well-written speech that highlighted his best qualities without lying about him. She didn't say that he would give you the shirt off his back or that his smile could light up a room. She did say that he had been a loyal friend and a passionate artist and that he had been larger than life. His father stood up, spoke a few poorly chosen words in laughable contrast to his ex-wife's speech, then, without warning, broke down in tears. The entire congregation was so stunned, no one moved or spoke for several minutes, and the only sound was his muffled, pitiful weeping. Finally, his wife went up to collect him and brought him back to their seats.

I was so disturbed by this unanticipated outburst, I hardly heard the remainder of the speeches, including LA's. Charlie didn't speak, of course. He'd barely spoken for a week. The only thing he said to me, in a whisper while the organ played *Amazing Grace*, was, "He would fucking hate this, Will." LA cried a few times throughout the service, and Lindsay cried too, though I wasn't sure if she was crying for Cynic or her brother. LA's parents were there and were nearly as inconsolable as poor Mr. Devereux. One would have thought their own son had died, and I thought that made up a bit for Cynic's mother's lack of emotion. Maybe, I reasoned to myself, she was too dead on the inside for tears, like Charlie. I didn't cry — I hadn't since the car ride with LA.

It was strange hearing Cynic's relatives speak of him as we awkwardly mingled over *hors d'oeuvres* after the service. They called him Cedric, of course, which I couldn't get used to. They told stories that didn't sound like Cynic at all, and I thought maybe they'd gotten him mixed up with one of his many cousins. The Christmas Eve he'd stayed up all night, determined to catch Santa Claus in the act, and they'd had to reveal the truth to him, but he'd never told the other kids. The time he'd gotten lost on a trip to the zoo and they'd searched for him for hours, only to find him sitting against the glass of the orangutan cage with the huge mother orangutan on the other side gazing at him as though she'd decided to adopt him. The time he'd climbed so high in a tree at the park because his cousin had dared him to, he'd gotten stuck, and they'd had to call the fire department to get him down, and he'd been so thrilled he'd devoted himself to becoming a firefighter for over a year. A new image of Cynic started to take shape in my mind, and I found it deeply unsettling. How much had I really known him? How much had he allowed me to see?

Perhaps the worst part was that everyone consumed at least a handful of drinks, toasting him and clinking their glasses together, then got in their cars and drove off. I couldn't wrap my mind around it. It would be like me smoking a pack a day after watching my father die with a tube in his throat. Did they think they were somehow impervious to sharing Cynic's fate? Did they think that because it was a funeral, they had a reason to drink, and they weren't alcoholics, so it didn't count? Perhaps it was this that upset my stomach, or perhaps it was one of the *hors d'oeuvres* I'd choked down, but I got so sick we had to go back to the hotel and I spent the night on the bathroom floor. Mr. Devereux had offered to let us stay at his house in the suburbs, and when we'd tactfully declined, he'd put us up at the Boston Park Plaza, proving himself a bit like his son after all.

I felt better in the morning, and while Charlie slept in, splayed across the enormous king bed, I took the bus to Boston University. The campus was everything I'd dreamed of when I'd envisioned going to school on the East Coast—picturesque old-world buildings, lush flowering trees, the velvety sapphire river and the air of quiet, sophisticated busyness found only in academia. I found there the same sense of timelessness that I'd experienced in Europe, the sense that I'd stepped through a window of history where everything that had ever happened was perfectly preserved, crystallized and untouchable.

I didn't mention the fact that it was my twenty-seventh birthday, and Charlie forgot. Cynic had died on his twenty-seventh birthday, and the number felt cursed to me now. We'd been able to reschedule our returning flight for that day. I wouldn't have minded hanging around Boston for a week, seeing all the places Cynic had wanted to show us, but Charlie was in no condition for that. He slept most of the time now and started to get tired and cranky after being up for a few hours, like a toddler. We went back to Weston, where the campus had emptied for spring break. Cynic's death had been met with widespread shock and staggering grief. He was loved, as public figures and gods are loved, by people who hardly knew him. It was impossible to go anywhere that first week without running into groups of crying girls and seeing the art students' tributes to him in chalk all over the sidewalk.

LA and Lindsay had gone back to California with LA's parents so Charlie and I were alone, and he wasn't much for company. He let me hold him sometimes, but he didn't hold me back so it felt a bit like cuddling a pillow for comfort. All other forms of physical affection were off limits. I tried to kiss him once, and he flinched away as though I'd struck him. I felt loneliness that week that I hadn't felt since community college when I'd rented that dingy basement room in the elderly couple's home. Every day I woke up next to him hoping he would roll over and nestle into the crook of my arm like he used to, and every day he didn't. I feared that he felt he couldn't talk to me about Cynic, that I hadn't been as adept at hiding my jealousy as I'd thought. I wanted to tell him that it was all right, that I didn't mind if he'd been in love with Cynic, or if he still was, and that I understood. But I couldn't bring myself to broach the topic. I didn't want him to flinch away from me again, or maybe I just didn't want to know the truth.

Charlie took sleeping pills at night and sometimes during the day. I'd thrown away the bottle I'd taken from him on that first night, but another bottle had appeared. I started counting them after he'd passed out, completely dead to the world, to keep track of how many he was taking. I went through his drawers and wardrobe to see if he had any more stashed away, but if he did I couldn't find them. He drank too — whenever he was awake long enough. It wasn't unusual for us to sip from a bottle of something or other while we read, or listened to music, or studied in his room. But I couldn't bear the taste or smell of liquor anymore — it made me physically ill — so whenever he pulled one of those bottles from under his bed, I retreated across the room and sulked.

I told him a dozen times not to mix those pills with liquor, but he wouldn't listen to me. I couldn't stop him, not without physically intervening, and I couldn't do that because I was afraid he would kick me out of his room. I knew he didn't want me there, but I dreaded leaving him alone. Even when I went out to do laundry or buy food, I hurried, shadowed by a black cloud of trepidation. I couldn't stop thinking about his suicidal ideation in his freshman year. Cynic had saved him by needing him, and now Cynic was gone. I wanted to show him that I needed him too — I needed him desperately. But I had an awful feeling that I didn't and would never need him quite as much as Cynic had.

Spring break seemed to drag on forever, but finally it ended. LA and Lindsay came back and started dress rehearsals for *Hamlet*. I tried to get Charlie to go watch them, but he wasn't interested, and I didn't want to go without him. We both went back to our classes, at least some of the time, though neither of us did much of the work. It didn't matter — our GPAs were safe, and we'd been accepted into our graduate programs, although Charlie never talked about Columbia anymore. We never set foot in the Blackbird again. I got us food from the cafeteria instead, which I practically had to beg him to eat. I couldn't even look at the café when I walked past it, for fear that I would see someone else sitting in our booth. I wondered if the school had made Cynic's parents pay off his tab or if they had let it slide.

I knew he was busy with his play, but I also got the sense that LA was avoiding us. It hurt me because I really could have used his help with Charlie. It scared me that Charlie didn't have anyone but me. I even thought of going through his phone while he was sleeping to get his mother's number. But I knew she was strictly Catholic, and I wasn't sure how she would feel about getting a call from her son's boyfriend. Perhaps she wouldn't even mind because she didn't think of him as a son at all, and that was worse.

On opening night, I went to see *Hamlet* alone. Charlie was so deeply asleep, I figured he wouldn't be able to inflict any more abuse on himself before I got back. Still, I worried, and the dark theme of the play didn't help at all. The theater was more packed than usual, and I spotted well-dressed, formidable-looking strangers in the crowd who were no doubt the long-awaited talent scouts. My stomach fluttered with secondhand nerves when LA appeared onstage. But he was marvelous as always... Until Act III when he got to the famed soliloquy.

"To be, or not to be, that is the question,
Whether 'tis nobler in the mind to suffer
The slings and arrows of outrageous fortune,
Or to take arms against a sea of troubles,
And by opposing end them?"

He paused dramatically, and the audience waited with bated breath. I found myself leaning forward in my seat. But something happened then. He stared into the crowd, face pale under the stage lights, and for the first time since I'd met him, LA froze. An agonizing moment dragged by, then another. A rustle went through the audience as people shifted in their chairs, exchanging glances and murmuring. It was something out of every stage actor's nightmares. At last, he turned and stumbled off the stage. The curtain fell, and the audience began to buzz with speculation. I got up and pushed my way to the aisle.

People were scrambling backstage. LA's understudy was shunted past me, half in costume, muttering the soliloquy under his breath. I asked around until I found LA alone in a dressing room, sitting at a makeup table, his face buried in his hands. He looked up at my reflection in the mirror as I entered. His face was drawn, eyes wide and stunned.

"Shit, I'm so sorry," he said. "I don't know what happened. That's never happened to me before."

It made my heart ache that he would think he had any reason to apologize to me. "It's okay, don't apologize. With everything that's happened lately, no one can blame you."

Pain lanced through his features. Then, to my astonishment, he burst out, "Why did he have to do this to me? He knew how important this play was—the most important role of my life so far. My whole career depends on impressing these talent scouts. And he had to fucking ruin it!" He blanched with horror at his own words, then buried his face in his hands again. "Fuck! Sorry, I know that was insanely selfish."

"Elijah," I said, stepping toward him. But no other words came to mind.

His shoulders shook as he drew in deep, shuddering breaths. "I just can't stop thinking it, Will," he said after a pause. "I just can't stop thinking... Did he do it on purpose? Was he trying to punish us?"

"No," I said with more confidence than I felt. "No, I really don't think so. I really don't think he would do that."

He nodded and swallowed hard. "I know. I just keep having the worst thoughts. That's why I'm staying away from Charlie. I'm afraid I'm going to say something awful in front of him, something I can't take back... How is he?"

I splayed my hands at my sides in a gesture of helplessness.

He looked at me in the mirror, a glaze of tears shimmering in his dark eyes. "This is so fucked up, Will."

It had, of course, occurred to me that Cynic might have taken his own life. I tried to shove these thoughts into the darkest corners of my mind, but the fact that LA was thinking them too made it harder. I thought of him nearly drinking himself to death their freshman year. I thought of his incessant smoking. I thought of him flinging open the French doors in Paris and stepping out onto the balcony — the mad notion I'd had that he was going to jump. I thought of Charlie telling me that Cynic was fragile. Should I have seen something like this coming? Had I failed him? Had he done what he did — at least in part — to punish me?

The guilt crept in, overpowering everything else I felt. Every negative thought I'd ever had about him, every pang of resentment, every time I'd been short with him rose to the surface of my mind. How I'd avoided him after that day in the practice room, ashamed by my rush of desire. How I'd snapped at him in Europe and told him Charlie and I didn't want him. What if we would have just done it? Would a ménage à trois have been so terrible? Would I have hated it that much? Could it have saved my relationship with Cynic? Could it have saved his life? My thoughts spiraled until I finally turned to drinking again. The taste of alcohol still made me sick, but at least it shut my brain up for a while.

Charlie's substance abuse was truly out of control. I found him passed out on the floor one night and couldn't wake him up for five minutes, and I nearly lost my mind. In fact, I did lose my mind. I threw his bottles of liquor out the window, hearing them smash on the sidewalk below. I could have killed someone. I grabbed his pills from the nightstand, he tried to wrestle them away from me, and I elbowed him in the face. I didn't mean to. He was so much smaller than me, and I'd never been so frightened by my own size. He sat down hard on the bed, fingers pressed to his bloody lip, and I dropped to my knees in front of him.

"Charlie, I'm so sorry. I'm so sorry. I didn't mean to. Please forgive me, Charlie."

He let me hug him around the waist and bury my head in his lap. He even ran his fingers through my hair. It was the first time he'd willingly touched me in weeks. We wound up lying in bed together, my arms wrapped tightly around him.

"Do you want to break up?" I asked him, hearing the tremor in my voice.

He didn't answer for a second, and my stomach plummeted. "No," he said finally. "Do you?"

"No," I said quickly, awash with relief. "But lately I feel like you don't want to be with me."

It took him a long time to answer again. "I do. But...I just don't think I can do it anymore. The boyfriend stuff. Sex, kissing, telling you everything. I just don't think I have it in me."

"That's okay," I insisted. "You don't have to do any of that stuff right now. I still want to be with you."

"Why?"

"Because I love you, Charlie."

He didn't say it back. He never did anymore.

Chapter Twelve

LA had dropped out of the play. He told me he'd tried to do the soliloquy again in rehearsal and had broken down crying. *Hamlet* ran its course and the talent scouts went on their way. But Lindsay, who had only had a small part in *Hamlet* but a large part in a simultaneous production of *Into the Woods*, got a call a week later. A small up-and-coming agency in New York wanted to sign her and fly her out immediately after graduation for a series of auditions. It was clear she was over the moon, but she tried to downplay it in front of LA so he wouldn't feel too bad. I still figured LA would get his big break soon enough after moving to New York—he was too talented not to. It came as a complete shock when he told me that he didn't think he was moving there after all.

"I was thinking I should go home for a while," he said as we meandered the campus one sunny afternoon. "Take a break from everything, you know? My brother said he can get me a job answering phones at his law office."

I was aghast. "But you always said you'd rather die than work a single day at a desk job. You're going to be miserable. Cyn wouldn't want that. I know that sounds corny, but he wouldn't."

"Well, maybe he shouldn't have left me then," he burst out, startling me and drawing the attention of several passersby. "If he cared about me, if he cared about what happens in my life, then maybe he should've stuck around."

I realized that he was now fully convinced that Cynic had taken his own life. I still hadn't made up my mind on the matter, but he had, and he was angry. "Elijah," I said carefully, "please think about this. I don't want Charlie to be alone in New York."

I saw his shoulders sag. We had stopped on the path under a waving oak tree with bright new leaves. "Lindsay's still going," he said with a sigh.

"But Charlie needs someone who knows him better. He needs someone who can take care of him." I couldn't bear to think of him alone in his dorm room at Columbia with his booze and his pills and his obvious death wish.

"Why can't you take care of him?" LA asked.

Truthfully, I had thought about giving up BU to follow Charlie to New York. I didn't know what I would do there. It would be terribly clingy and pathetic, but I'd thought about it nonetheless. "I don't think he wants me to," I confessed.

His hair fell silkily over his forehead as he hung his head. "I'm sorry. But I can't take care of Charlie. I can barely take care of myself."

An ache rose in my throat at the thought of him living all the way across the country from me. I hadn't realized how much I was relying on LA being only a few hours' drive away. I was overwhelmed by my fondness for him all at once, which was so much simpler and so much deeper than my love for Cynic had been. "I'll miss you," I said thickly.

He looked up in alarm at my sudden display of emotion. "Will, I'll miss you too! And we'll still see each other all the time, I swear. I'll visit you, and Lindsay and Charlie, and you'll all come visit me, right?"

"Right," I agreed, blinking back unexpected tears. It was amazing the things I could sit through stoically, and the things that made me cry like a baby.

He hugged me, soft hair brushing my chin. I forgot how short he was sometimes — his personhood was so vast.

My mother didn't come to graduation, which wasn't surprising because I hadn't invited her. Charlie's mother didn't come either. But I looked into the crowd at one point and was astounded to see Cynic's mother there, like a stately apparition, and the sight of her put some unquiet part of my mind at rest because I finally had the confirmation I needed that she had loved him. LA's entire family was there, and they behaved as though Charlie and I were their own, for which I was immeasurably grateful. I crossed the stage to the sound of their uproarious cheering and felt as though I did have a family. Charlie crossed the stage shortly after me, moving like a sleepwalker. He was sober, at least — I'd made sure of that. There was a moment of silence for Cynic toward the end, and they played a recording of one of his piano pieces. This one wasn't as dark and hypnotic as most of his compositions — it was light and pretty, and I was certain he'd done it as an assignment for a class. Still, I was glad that his mother got the chance to hear it after missing his concerts year after year.

We went out to dinner with the Inoue family afterward—I made Charlie go—and the atmosphere was so cheery that I was almost able to forget that we would all be going our separate ways the next day—Charlie and Lindsay to New York, LA and his family to California, and me to Boston. I'd found a room to rent and another job tutoring summer school kids, and I was looking forward to getting to know my new home. Without discussing it, Charlie and I had agreed not to spend the summer together. I talked of visiting him on the weekends, and of us going to Portland to visit Mara and Valerie, and California to visit LA, but I knew deep down that it wasn't going to happen. We weren't really together anymore. We hadn't actually broken up, but I could tell we weren't together by the way he avoided my gaze like he had in those early days as if looking at me were somehow dangerous.

I went to help him pack his things even though he hadn't asked me to—his clothes, his notebooks, his guitar, his sheaves of music and his countless books. He would be staying with Lindsay in her new apartment, where she'd intended to live with LA, until he could move into the dorms at Columbia that fall. I was intensely grateful to her, though she claimed it was convenient because she needed a roommate and didn't know anyone else in New York. I had taken her aside to tell her about his substance abuse and my fears about his suicidal tendencies, which I worried might be triggering for her after her brother's death. But, to my slight surprise, she told me that she loved Charlie, that he had always been her favorite out of LA's friends and that as long as she had the ability to help him in any way, she would.

I spent the night without asking him if it was okay — I was afraid he would say no. I couldn't sleep so I lay awake listening to the sound of his breathing and thinking that it was the most important sound I would ever hear, more important than music, or laughter, or the lap of the lake on the shore or any of the other essential sounds that had come to define my life in the past two years. I decided that it was all right if Charlie didn't want to be with me anymore, that I could live with it, as long I knew he was out there somewhere in the world, still breathing. Even if he never wanted to see me again, that was okay as long as he kept living.

His flight was in the morning and mine was in the afternoon, so I waited around to help him carry his things down to Lindsay's car even though I hadn't started my own packing yet. He sat on his bare mattress as we waited for her to arrive, gazing out the window and fiddling with a loose thread unraveling from the sleeve of his hoodie. I watched him, trying to store every detail of his image in my memory — the perfect little swirls of hair at his temples, the defined shapes of his jawline and chin, the thin golden frames of his glasses and the blue light from the window reflected in the panes.

"Charlie," I said, hearing the way my voice went soft around his name, the way my tongue caressed each syllable. He must've been able to hear it too because he winced. I didn't tell him I loved him. I had already said it so many times, and each time he seemed to shrink a little as if I were draining his life force. Instead, I said, "Listen. If you ever need me…if you ever feel like hurting yourself or…or just want to talk, you call me, okay? I don't care if we're not together anymore. I don't care if we haven't seen each other in a long time. I don't care if it's the middle of the night. You still call me. Got it?"

I thought I saw a trace of weakness flit across his face, like a fault line, and I fantasized briefly that he would break down and sob in my arms like I'd wanted him to all this time. I had still never seen him cry. But he composed himself and the fault line vanished, leaving a glassy but impenetrable shield of diamond. "Got it," he said quietly.

Lindsay arrived, and we all carried Charlie's things down together and loaded them into her car. He let me hug him before he left and buried his face in my shoulder for a minute. But when we drew apart, his eyes were still dry. Lindsay hugged me too, and her eyes were less dry. Then they drove off, and I stood there watching with my arms at my sides until the car was out of sight. I went back to my dorm room and cried myself into a hiccupping stupor. Then I packed my things — my books, my old flannels, my worn jeans, my cheap shoes that Cynic had mocked in Europe and all the knick-knacks I'd acquired throughout our travels — seashells from California, a *Hamilton* program from New York, a glitzy little keychain of the Statue of Liberty, another one of the Eiffel Tower, the euros I'd saved because they made me feel worldly and a lock I'd bought with Charlie before we realized that people couldn't leave locks on the Pont des Arts anymore.

I rode to the airport with LA and his family because I'd sold my junky Toyota. We again promised to visit each other soon and to go to New York to see our partners because I didn't have the heart to tell him that Charlie and I had broken up. I did think of it as a break-up now, even though we still hadn't said the words. LA hugged me before we parted for our respective destinations, and I clutched him tightly, pressing my lips to his hair as if I were trying to make up for the goodbye I hadn't had with Charlie and would never have with Cynic. That was how I left Michigan.

When I landed in Boston, I was overtaken by the strange sense that the past two years had been some sort of accidental detour. After all, I'd originally intended to go to college on the East Coast and hadn't wanted to linger in the Midwest any longer. But then, Weston hadn't been any of our first choices for our undergraduate studies. Charlie, Cynic, LA and I had all ended up there by chance. I felt as though I'd experienced some sort of time glitch and was actually eighteen, heading off to my first year of college, like I should have, to Boston University where I would perhaps meet an eighteen-year-old, somewhat less jaded Cynic.

I had a good summer, though I thought often of Charlie and of the previous summer we'd shared at the rented house on Lake Michigan—him saying, "*Have a good day,*" before I left in the mornings, lying on the dock together while the sun toasted our skin, the way he'd laughed when I told him that I'd thought he was dying, and that earth-shattering first kiss. I restrained myself from calling him or showing up unannounced at his door, but I did send texts, every day at first, then less often, which he almost never replied to. I kept in regular contact with Lindsay, who assured me daily, then weekly, that Charlie was fine. I went for long walks along the Charles River and lurked about the BU campus, and Harvard and MIT—I loved academia so. I tried to put all that love into my tutoring sessions, and

I hoped I got at least one or two high school kids excited about college.

By the end of the summer, I had decided that I didn't regret any of it—staying in my hometown to help care for my father, working at the general store, going to community college, and least of all going to Weston. All of it had led me to where I was now and the person I had become, and I wouldn't change it for anything. So, I started grad school at BU in the fall without a trace of bitterness clinging to me. I did, however, drop the appellation "Iowa" forever. I thought of Cynic more than I did of Charlie on that magnificent, melancholy, storybook campus that reminded me so much of him. I even fancied that I caught sight of him sometimes, rounding a corner, the tail of his black greatcoat swishing behind him, disappearing in a swirl of cigarette smoke, haunting the field of my peripheral vision.

I finally reconnected with my mother because I now understood what had driven her away from me—the shared grief, the terribleness of what we had endured together and the constant reminder of what we were to each other. That weight would always exist between us, but there were ways to navigate it, to lighten the burden for one another, and it would get easier over time. I wished the same could be true for Charlie and me. After each of my long, hard, cathartic conversations with her, the temptation to call him and continue was almost irresistible. But I knew Charlie had his own way of grieving, and I couldn't force him to share mine.

Even as I fell into my studies with a fervor that I never had before and found all the joy I'd been looking for in teaching my undergrad classes, a faint, niggling fear lingered at the back of my mind. It was the fear of a phone call in the middle of the night, a call that would flip the world upside down, LA or Lindsay's hollow voice saying, "Will...it's Charlie..." I plugged my phone in religiously every night and kept it on full volume on my nightstand. Every morning, I snatched it to stare at the screen until my eyes focused and showed me that I hadn't missed a call. But somehow, miraculously, months went by and I never got that call. Charlie kept living. And eventually, I had to accept the bittersweet truth that he hadn't left me because he was going to kill himself. He had left me because he didn't want me anymore.

Epilogue

A year later, shortly after I started my job as an English lit professor at a community college, I found out that an off-Broadway theater in New York was staging Charlie's musical about Amelio Robles Ávila. A Latino trans man was starring as Robles, of course. That weekend, I drove to New York to see it and sat in the back of the crowded theater. It was even more amazing than I could have envisioned, startlingly funny, with Robles swaggering about the stage and twirling his pistol, and powerfully moving. I remembered Charlie saying, *"For once, a trans person got a happy ending. I think that's an important story to tell,"* and I wept unabashedly at the final scene of Robles expiring peacefully in bed at the age of ninety-five. I looked for Charlie's curled mop in the audience but didn't see it, although I supposed it was possible that he had changed his hair.

Some months after that, I returned to New York to see Lindsay's first Broadway performance, starring in *Cats*. LA was there—he and Lindsay weren't together anymore but were still close friends—and the three of us went out for drinks afterward, giddy and elated, talking in feverish bursts about the old days. Charlie wasn't there, although LA mentioned that he had met him for coffee the day before, and Lindsay mentioned that he still came to most of her shows. I tried not to reveal how hurt I was. I had hoped that he and I might at least become friends again, after everything, but it seemed he no longer wanted me in his life at all.

I dated people, briefly and casually — a few women, a cis man, and a trans man who was very patient with me and taught me things I hadn't known before. It seemed I would never be done learning. But I didn't fall in love with anyone, and I began to suspect that I would carry a torch for Charlie for the rest of my life. I also made friends — best friends even — although LA remained my dearest friend even when I didn't hear from him for a while.

LA had a hard time in those couple years after Cynic died. I didn't realize how hard, caught up in my own life as I was. I didn't visit him as much as I'd promised I would, and sometimes we went weeks without talking. If I'd paid closer attention, perhaps I might have noticed that something was amiss. He crashed his car, driving drunk, almost two years to the day we'd lost Cynic. I didn't find out until a few days later, from Lindsay — there was no phone call in the middle of the night. No one was seriously hurt, and he checked himself into rehab afterward. I sent him texts and emails and tried to call, but he didn't respond. He must have been horribly ashamed.

A few months later, he called to tell me he was in Boston, and I dropped everything to drive to meet him. I lived out in the suburbs now where it was cheaper and quieter — Cynic would've judged me for it. We met at the Public Gardens and strolled the pretty green pathways under the willow trees, stopping to watch ducks and swans glide their way across the water. He looked healthy. He'd put on a little weight since the last time I'd seen him. But he wasn't the lively, animated LA I used to know. He told me about the twelve-step program he was doing and how it required him to apologize to the people he'd hurt.

I said, "Well, I hope you're not planning to apologize to me." He was always apologizing to me for nonsensical reasons, and I was always trying to get him to stop.

"Actually," he replied, "I was thinking about apologizing to Charlie. I wasn't there for him back then, you know? I wasn't a very good friend." He paused reflectively. "But I don't have his new number, and you know he was never one for social media. I suppose I could try sending him an email."

I stared at him in confusion. I had assumed he and Charlie were still in touch. "He changed his number?" I asked.

"Well, yeah, of course. Didn't you know? Charlie moved to London in May. He signed with an agency there. One of his plays is running on the West End."

I couldn't speak for a minute. At last, I choked out, "I didn't know."

"Sorry," he said, then smiled at himself for apologizing to me yet again.

I had become so reliant on the idea of Charlie being in New York, within driving distance, just in case he ever needed me, the knowledge that he was now living half a world away rattled me more than I could say. I couldn't help but think of how terribly long it would take me to get to London if I ever needed to—if I ever got that call that I no longer expected but still feared. It was silly, of course. Charlie didn't need me, and at some point I was going to have to admit that he never would. He wasn't a tragedy waiting to happen, he wasn't made of glass or paper, he wasn't one of those insects that only lived for a day, and he wasn't Brandon Teena from *Boys Don't Cry.* Charlie was going to be fine. He was well on his way to his happy ending.

That fall, LA got discovered. He'd been working at his brother's law office and hadn't done any acting in ages. But, by chance, one of the law firm's clients had a daughter who loved musicals, particularly *Newsies,* and had been obsessed with LA's performance as Jack Kelly back in the day. She'd been following him on social media ever since, even though he wasn't very active anymore. She recognized him on sight, and her father was a TV producer. Soon enough, LA landed himself a recurring role on a teen drama series — he was still so youthful-looking — as "the token Asian" (his words). The show was a bit over-the-top sometimes, but I still enjoyed it, and I loved seeing him back in his element.

Turning thirty was strange for me. My birthdays were always strange, ever since Cynic. Yet it somehow came as a relief too. I had made it through the turbulence of my twenties, and I felt it would be smooth sailing from here on out, though deep down I knew I was kidding myself. I had recently accepted an associate professorship in the English Department at the University of Massachusetts Boston and was working to obtain my doctorate. I was finally, by all rights, an adult. I celebrated it that night with my friends and the woman I'd been seeing. I was worn out by the time I went to bed. I couldn't party like I used to anymore. Even two glasses of wine were enough to give me a hangover these days. Still, I plugged in my phone and made sure the sound was on. It was a habit I figured I would never fully break.

That night, I finally got it — the call that flipped the world upside down. I knew with a cold, calm certainty the moment I woke to the clattering ringtone and blinding screen that it would be LA or Lindsay calling to tell me that Charlie was gone. I was so certain I didn't even look at the number when I answered it.

"Will?" said a soft, breathy voice on the other end.

My brain sluggishly processed the sound, then I sat bolt upright. "Charlie? Is that you?"

"Yeah." His voice was raw like he'd been drinking whiskey or crying. "I just wanted to say happy birthday."

I struggled to absorb this and to shake off the obliterating grief that had consumed me the instant I'd heard the phone ring. "Okay."

There was a pause, in which I heard him breathing shakily. I'd never thought I would have the chance to hear that precious sound again. "Listen," he said after a minute. "I know it's really late there, and this call is going to cost a fortune, but I was just hoping we could talk."

"Yeah," I said, scrambling out of bed with the phone pressed to my ear the same way I had on that awful night three years ago, except this time I was heading for my laptop to book the soonest possible flight to London. "Yeah, Charlie, of course we can talk."

At first, the conversation was awkward and uncertain, full of accidental interruptions and potent pauses. But after a while, it started to flow. We didn't talk about the past — there was too much to catch up on. Still, the past was there, underneath our words, heavy and bittersweet. It was so surreal to hear his voice again, I found myself questioning whether I was dreaming and had to get up and pace my room to convince myself I was awake. The first time he laughed—at some stupid joke I'd made—I felt an alarming twinge in my chest. It was a feeling I'd practically forgotten because it had been so long since I'd last felt it. That was when I knew that although everything was different now, one thing had remained the same.

It took me hours to work up the courage, and gray light was beginning to creep across the floor of my bedroom when I asked, my voice husky with nerves, "Are you seeing anyone?"

There was the briefest silence—I'd caught him by surprise—but to me, it seemed to last an eternity. Then he answered, "No. Not since you. I had some things to work through on my own." He hesitated. "What about you?"

I was so overcome with relief, I almost forgot for a second that I was seeing someone. I supposed I owed her a phone call. A text wouldn't cut it. "Yeah, I've been seeing someone," I admitted, already trying to formulate how I would break the news to her.

He didn't speak for a minute, and when he did, his voice was thick with emotion. "Will, I wanted to call sooner. I just had to make sure I was ready. If it's too late, I—"

I interrupted him, "Charlie, I don't love her. I mean it. I haven't loved anyone else. I still..." I broke off, suddenly unsure if this was the right moment for such a confession. But he caught my meaning.

"Still?" he asked me.

At that moment, I caught sight of the digital clock on my nightstand and realized I still needed to pack a bag. "Can we keep talking about this later?" I asked, balancing the phone on my shoulder as I plunged into my closet for an armful of clothes. "I have a flight to catch."

"Oh." He sounded startled and faintly disappointed. "Where are you going?"

"London," I replied, heaving my suitcase down from the top shelf.

I heard his breath catch and could vividly picture the expression on his face — the dumbfounded look he used to give me whenever I took a dramatic leap in our relationship. "Will," he exclaimed with a note of disbelief.

"I know," I said, packing haphazardly and wondering if I was out of my mind. "I know it's too much. But this is who I am, okay?" I had always, from the very beginning, been too much for Charlie. But he had loved me in spite of that, or perhaps because of it, and if there was even the smallest chance he still did, I had to grab that chance before it could slip through my fingers.

He let out a shaky little laugh. "Okay," he said, once again accepting me for the reckless, shameless, hopeless romantic I was. "I'm glad you haven't changed."

Want to see more like this?
Here's a taster for you to enjoy!

Out in Austin: Teddy's Truth
KD Ellis

Excerpt

Teddy tugged at the hem of his overlarge sweatshirt then discreetly scratched beneath the band of his sticky sports bra. As far as he was concerned, breasts were disgusting lumps of fat that hoarded sweat, bounced like painful beanbags on his chest when he was busy catching a football and strained the front of any button-down he tried to wear. He couldn't understand why boys were so obsessed with them. He personally couldn't wait to get the damn things cut off.

Hormone therapy had deepened his voice and given him a shadow of patchy fuzz on his jaw. Clippers had sheared him of his blond hair and his mother's Italian heritage had blessed him with broad shoulders and narrow hips.

It was unfortunate that it had also cursed him with breasts that not even puberty blockers had been able to thwart.

He wished he could blame her awful time-management skills on their heritage as well, but he knew better. The fault lay with either Jack or John – the bottle or the boyfriend, whichever she was currently in bed with.

He'd been sitting on the hard, concrete steps of the high school for almost an hour. It wasn't like he could call her. His cell was out of minutes, and hers was probably dead on the nightstand.

Just as the final school bus trundled back onto the parking lot and Teddy was about to give up on waiting, someone stepped up beside him, casting him in shadow.

"Stay there," Teddy ordered, craning his head back until he could grin at his best friend. "Perfect. Be my sun block."

Shiloh, still in his leotard, laughed and nudged Teddy's hip with his shoe. "If you don't think I shine brighter than the sun, then clearly I'm not wearing enough glitter."

"Shine as bright as you want, but just keep standing there. Fuck, it's hot!" Teddy gripped his collar and tugged at it repeatedly, trying to stir a breeze. All it ended up doing was wafting the stench of boob sweat up into his face.

"Well, duh, it's ninety degrees—and you're in a sweater." Shiloh rolled his eyes and dropped onto the curb beside him. "And it's not even pink."

Teddy opened his mouth, his usual response dancing on his tongue—that boys don't wear pink—but he swallowed it. Shiloh was currently in a hot pink leotard and pink Chucks.

Instead, Teddy shrugged and glared down at his baggy jeans and boring blue sweater. "You know why." It was hard enough getting people to call him Teddy instead of Thea. Or, worse, Theodora.

"I'm going to make you a shirt. It's going to be pink and fabulous. It's going to say, 'Call Me Teddy'. *And* it's going to be in glitter." Shiloh threw an imaginary handful into the air, then fell back to lie on the sidewalk, his arms flung out.

"With your handwriting, they'd probably think you wrote 'Daddy'." Teddy dropped back to use Shiloh's arm as a pillow.

Shiloh shifted but didn't pull away. He just rolled onto his side, his blond hair flopping into his eyes. He left his arm beneath Teddy's head, bringing their faces close enough that their noses nearly touched. "It's not *that* bad. Besides, you're clearly not a *Daddy*."

Teddy rolled his eyes. Ever since he'd borrowed Shiloh's laptop to finish up his college application essays — and forgotten to clear his search history after falling down the rabbit hole of kinky porn — Shiloh's teasing had been less than subtle. Teddy refused to be embarrassed, though, especially since the only reason he'd stumbled onto that website in the first place was because Shiloh had left three separate bookmarks for it.

It reinforced everything Teddy knew about their relationship. They were destined to be the bestest of friends — but nothing more. They were both too attracted to the same type of man — tall, dark and dangerous.

Still, knowing his friend was into the same kinks that he was didn't mean they needed to talk about it. He ignored the leading comment and switched back to the far safer topic of handwriting. "Remember when Mr. Carmine thought you wrote an essay on *Storage Wars*?"

"Hey, Mr. Carmine also thought you wrote an essay about Quasimodo."

"I did write him an essay about Quasimodo. Well, really about how the novel by Victor Hugo helped raise the money needed to restore the cathedral, and —" Teddy felt the beginnings of a spiel on gothic architecture creeping up.

Shiloh interrupted, "Yeah, buttresses...a rose window. I remember. I still think the gargoyles are creepy."

"You said buttresses," Teddy snickered, shoving Shiloh's shoulder.

"Teddy, can I touch your *buttress*?"

"Your hand can stay far away from my *buttress*, fuck you very much."

"It's like a butt fortress. I just want to invade your buttress! Why are you so mean to me?" Shiloh rolled onto his back and kicked his feet against the sidewalk like an angry toddler, except for the smile on his face.

"No, it's impregnable!" Teddy stuck out his tongue.

"Well, duh, you're a boy. Of course you're impregnable."

"Something tells me you don't know what that word means."

Immediately, Shiloh rattled off the definition. "Impregnable. Unable to be captured or broken into. Also, unable to be defeated or destroyed. But you have to admit that it sounds an awful lot like it means you can't make babies."

"And thank God for that," Teddy shivered at the thought of being responsible for a little, squalling, helpless baby. "I might miss wearing pink, but I won't miss *that*."

Teddy froze at the accidental admission. His therapist had told him that it was normal, that gender was a spectrum and that just because he still liked feminine things didn't make his desire to transition less valid. Still, it was the first time he'd admitted it to anyone except his therapist.

Shiloh sat up slightly to face him better. "You can still wear pink. You can wear whatever the fuck you want." Shiloh's voice hardened. "And if anyone bothers you about it, I'll cover their lockers in gay porn. Just say the word."

"The poor football players won't know what to do with themselves. Think of all the spontaneous erections." The few he'd dated had been far more interested in his ass than a straight guy probably should be — not that he'd obliged, since he refused to be anyone's dirty little secret.

Shiloh sighed. "It would be a beautiful gift to all of us."

A black Mercedes pulled up to the curb, barely parking before the driver was leaning on the horn.

"Impatient bastard," Shiloh grumbled. "I don't know why he's in a hurry. He gets paid by the hour."

"Well, that stick is so far up his ass it has to be uncomfortable sitting down." Teddy sat up and straightened his sweatshirt. The Becketts' driver was a homophobic dick. He didn't understand how the man hadn't been fired yet.

Shiloh pushed himself to his feet. "I bet he has hemorrhoids. That's probably where he rushes off to every night."

"Ew. You picture him rubbing cream on his ass?" Teddy teased.

Shiloh gagged, shoving Teddy to the side. "Gross. You're such a dick. I don't know why I hang out with you."

"Because you love me."

The Mercedes blared its horn again, a demanding series of honks that only ended when Shiloh threw a hand up in acknowledgment. "I gotta go. Do you have a ride?"

Teddy shrugged. "Yeah. She must just be running late or something. I'm sure she'll be here soon." He knew she wouldn't be, but he'd rather walk than listen to the driver sling slurs. He didn't understand how Shiloh dealt with it.

Shiloh hesitated on the bottom step, looking like he wanted to say something, but all he did was give a small nod and say, "Okay. See you Monday?"

"Yeah, see you."

About the Author

Kai Wolden writes fantasy, sci fi, and contemporary fiction starring queer, trans, and gender-nonconforming characters. Whether it takes place in outer space, a fantasy world, or a modern-day college campus, Kai loves honest, heart-wrenching stories about queer love in all its forms: friendship, romance, found family, and those ambiguous relationships that are somewhere in-between. Growing up queer and trans in small-town Wisconsin, Kai always wished he could find fictional characters who were more like him. Now he's populating the world with them, one book at a time!

Kai loves to hear from readers. You can find his contact information, website details and author profile page at https://www.pride-publishing.com

P U B L I S H I N G

Sign up for our newsletter and find out about all our
romance book releases, eBook sales and promotions,
sneak peeks and FREE romance books!

CPSIA information can be obtained
at www.ICGtesting.com
Printed in the USA
JSHW060742290722
28478JS00001B/61